## CONTENTS

**Hartwick Publishing**

Boss Woman

# 1

Fuck.

How did this happen?

The day started off so normal. Her panties were sitting in my pocket, we were text-flirting back and forth, and then out of nowhere, a bomb was dropped.

It destroyed everything.

Titan gave me the benefit of the doubt to get things cleared up with the reporter. She was pissed beyond reason, but she had the logic to hear me out. She still had enough affection for me to give me a little bit of room to make my case.

But all that went out the window when she saw the files sitting in my bottom drawer.

There was no coming back from that.

It was incriminating as hell. It was the smoking gun, the physical proof that I'd snooped around in her business. When I said I got the information but never looked at it, even I could barely believe myself. There was no way a smart woman like Tatum Titan would buy it.

I was in such deep shit.

I didn't know what to do.

I didn't know where to begin.

How did I fix this?

I started at the *New York Times*. I walked into the building and asked for Jared Newman. After waiting for nearly forty-five minutes, I was finally taken to his office. This guy was just a faceless name, but I wanted to murder him right in front of dozens of witnesses. "Why did you name me as the source in your article?" I didn't introduce myself or make small talk. Getting myself vindicated was the only chance I had to get Titan back.

He looked at me over his desk, slightly timid by the ferocity in my gaze. He looked like a typical reporter, wearing a light blue collared shirt with glasses. He was in his early forties, his eyes beginning to crinkle around the corners. "Because you were the source— and you told me I could name you."

"When?" I hissed. "You and I have never spoken. We've never even emailed each other. Who did you speak to?"

"You," he said in a bored voice. "At least, that's what I was told at the time."

"Did this happen over the phone?" I should take a seat but I couldn't. I was far too maniacal not to stand. There was so much adrenaline, so much destruction inside my veins. I wanted to trash his office the way I just trashed mine.

"Yes."

"When? I want all the details."

"Three days ago. You called at four in the afternoon, said you were Diesel Hunt, and told me your story. Told me to name you as the source. You sent me a packet of documents from the police department to prove your story."

Someone was out to get me. But who? "Don't you have a process to actually check your sources before you name them? I never called you. I never sent anything. Someone else impersonated me. I'm being framed here."

"Framed?" he asked. "You aren't being accused of a crime."

"Tatum Titan is my business partner. She thinks I threw her under the bus when I didn't. This has to be cleared up."

Jared shrugged like he didn't know what to do. "All the information checked out, and the papers said they were from you. The damage has been done. The story is all over the news. What am I supposed to do? I can't write another article just to say the source was unknown, not you."

"Damn right, you can."

"No one is going to read it. And we aren't going to print our mistake."

"Don't you think there's a story in this mysterious person who went through all of this?" I pressed. "Don't you think there's a story to tell there?"

"Give me evidence, and I'll look into it. So far, you haven't given me any proof that it wasn't you that I spoke to. Now that you're taking heat, maybe you've changed your mind about the whole thing. You want me to clear your name when you still did the crime."

I had to remind myself murder was illegal. I couldn't kill this guy without spending the rest of my life in jail.

"The best I can do is call Tatum Titan and explain to her that there's a possibility someone posed as you when they gave me this information."

"It's gotta be better than that." I could pay anyone to call her and pretend to be a reporter. That won't mean shit to Titan.

He shrugged again. "Then there's nothing else I

can do. Unless you provide substantial evidence that your suspicion is right, I can't print anything else."

"You know what you could do?" I clenched my jaw as I stared at him. "You can make sure you get the right source next time. What is this? A high school newspaper?" I stormed out of his office and tried to break the door when I slammed it.

I was exactly where I started—at the bottom.

⸻

WHEN I REACHED HER BUILDING, THERE WERE A DOZEN reporters outside. Like zookeepers waiting for a wild animal to emerge, they had their nets and cages ready. They wanted to swarm Titan the second she made an appearance and bombard her with questions she didn't want to answer.

Ridiculous.

Being seen walking into her building would just give them something new to print, so I returned to the back seat of my car and called her.

No answer.

"Fuck." I tried again.

No answer.

I rested my head against the dark leather and closed my eyes, feeling the sinking sensation inside my chest. I felt weaker than I ever had. My entire life was a mess, and I didn't know how to fix it. Titan wouldn't speak to me, and I knew it would be an uphill battle just to get her to listen to me for one minute.

I didn't know what to do.

If it were me, I wouldn't even return to my penthouse. She must know about the reporters huddled outside. She probably checked in to a hotel room or was staying with someone.

That thought made me think of Thorn.

She was probably with him.

I had Thorn's number, so I called him. I didn't expect the conversation to go well. I didn't even expect to get what I wanted. But I had to start somewhere.

It rang three times before he answered. When he spoke, he sounded more menacing than I'd ever heard him. Our mutual jealousy over one another seemed like high school drama compared to the threat in his tone. "The only reason you are alive right now is because I haven't figured out how to get away with murder."

I didn't doubt him, not when he'd actually killed someone once before. But the threat meant nothing to me when all I cared about was Titan. "I didn't do it, Thorn."

"Give it up, jackass."

"I didn't," I repeated. "I just went down to the *Times* and—"

"I don't care. Titan doesn't care. The only reason why I answered the phone is so I can give you our stance on the situation. You are officially our biggest nemesis. You are marked as our enemy. And you're about to find out what we do to our enemies."

"Thorn—"

"Titan will meet you at Stratosphere tomorrow morning. You'll come to an agreement on what to do with the company. In the meantime, don't bother either one of us. You've done enough."

Click.

## 2

TITAN

REPORTERS WERE PESTERING me left and right, and new articles were surfacing on the internet. My worst nightmare was becoming a reality, and I prayed people wouldn't dig any deeper. I could live with the scar the public was painting on me, as much as it killed me, but I couldn't let this ruin Thorn.

Not when he was the only person in the world I could trust.

He deserved better.

I stayed at his penthouse because I couldn't go back to mine. Reporters camped out there overnight, waiting for the chance to interview me. Even getting a glimpse of me on camera was good publicity for them. Just when my image had reached new heights, it came crashing down all over again.

I was livid with Hunt, so angry that I didn't have a

chance to feel the heartbreak that was bound to follow. Above all else, I felt so goddamn stupid. He lured me right into the trap, and I fell for it.

How could I let this happen?

How I could I trust him so easily?

Thorn hung up the phone and tossed it on the table, not caring about the livelihood of his device. He sighed and massaged his wrist, a habit he'd had for years. He needed to do something with his hands when he was angry, to concentrate on something so he wouldn't explode.

I didn't ask about the conversation because I heard every single word. Hunt continued to proclaim he was innocent even though the writing was on the wall. He'd already made a fool of us once, and now he was trying to do it again.

Not gonna happen.

My glass was firmly in my grasp, the ice cubes getting the surface cold. I set it down because it was empty. I was too depressed for another drink—and that was a first for me. "Thorn...I'm so sorry." I closed my eyes, so ashamed that I couldn't look at him. "I never wanted this to happen to you. I never should have told him..."

"Titan."

I didn't open my eyes.

"Titan," he repeated.

I took a deep breath before I looked at him, squaring my shoulders and appearing as strong as possible.

Thorn flashed me his merciless stare. "Don't apologize to me. Tatum Titan doesn't apologize to anyone."

"But I'm not Tatum Titan right now. I'm just Tatum when I'm with you. I could handle this so much better if it affected only me. But I know how bad this could be for you."

"It's going to be fine," he said confidently. "There's not enough evidence to pin anything on me. Even if Hunt is trying to incriminate me, he doesn't have any evidence. He only has what you said. Even if he recorded you, he can't use it in a court of law. And if a jury ever were to ask you what happened that night, I know you would cover for me. There's nothing to be worried about."

I suspected this wasn't over. I suspected this nightmare was only beginning.

"This is how we're going to handle this," Thorn said. "You're gonna go on about your life with your head held high. You aren't going to stop going to work. You are only going to take one interview, one that really matters. You aren't going to lie about what happened. But you're gonna make everyone feel like shit for ever asking you about it."

The last thing I wanted to do was talk about it. Now everyone was painting me as a domestic violence victim. I used to be a symbol of strength for women everywhere. I didn't put up with bullshit, ever. I held my head high. Knowing I ever let someone defeat me emotionally and physically was devastating to everyone. How could I be a champion to the world?

"You're going to change the narrative," Thorn said. "You're gonna come out on top. Don't worry about it."

"I don't know about that...everyone is judging me as we speak."

"And we're gonna make them feel like shit for doing it. You're going to prove to everyone how strong you are. You're going to prove to everyone that you can still come out on top even when you start at the bottom. If anything, this is going to make you an even bigger role model, Titan. You'll see."

"I hope so..." Even if we could bury this, it didn't change the biggest issue in my life. My business partner betrayed me. The man I fell in love with never loved me. His only interest in me was to destroy me. It was only a matter of time before he told the world about our arrangement, that my relationship with

Thorn was nothing but a big hoax. He was going to destroy my reputation. He was going to burn me alive.

I wanted to kill him.

"You had Hunt sign an NDA, right?" Thorn asked.

I closed my eyes.

Thorn knew the answer. "Shit."

"He refused to sign it...said we didn't need it."

"Fuck, this nightmare just keeps getting worse."

Now I knew why he didn't sign it. Now I knew it was his goal all along.

"You're meeting him tomorrow. Buy him out even if he price-gouges you. Just get rid of him. You want me to be there?"

I put on a brave face, but I was broken underneath. It would be so much easier to let Thorn handle this. But I couldn't let Hunt know he ruined me. I couldn't give him the satisfaction of victory. I'd been demolished a lot in my life, but I always put the pieces back together and built myself back up. This would be no different. I would look him in the eye, wear my hardest expression, and show him he didn't make a single dent in my hard exterior. "No. I can handle it."

"You're sure?"

"Yes." I was Tatum Titan. Nothing could destroy me. I could do this.

I WAS PURPOSELY LATE, WASTING HUNT'S TIME intentionally.

The elevator doors opened, and I walked onto the floor where our four assistants sat. They all looked at me differently, every single one of them having read the article from top to bottom.

I was going to get this look a lot, so I had to deal with it. "Morning, ladies." I walked by them and into the conference room, my stilettos tapping against the floor as I walked absolutely straight. My posture was perfect, my outfit was sophisticated, and I wore a slight smile like today was just like every other day.

Hunt stood in front of the floor-to-ceiling windows, his hands in his pockets. His ass looked tight in his slacks, and his jacket fit over his broad shoulders precisely. Slim in the hips and broad across the back, he was the same masculine man he was before.

But I refused to feel anything.

My stilettos announced my presence.

Hunt spun around and looked at me with those mocha-colored eyes, the ones that used to stare at me when we were in bed together. He still wore that look of devastation, like this was all as much of a surprise to him as it was to me. "Tatum—"

"I prefer Titan, Mr. Hunt." I took a seat at the head of the table and opened my folder. "Please take a seat so we can get started." I didn't look up as I organized my things, treating him like any other client I had to deal with. I'd dealt with assholes all my life, and I did it with the kind of poise that only annoyed them more. Hunt was no different.

He moved swiftly across the room and dropped into the chair on my right. He leaned forward, invading my space with his magnetic field. "I talked to the reporter, and he said he spoke with me over the phone. Apparently, 'I' mailed him the police reports, and that was why—"

"I'm here to discuss business, Mr. Hunt. Nothing else." I pulled the first page from my folder and placed it in front of him. "This is my offer."

"Your offer for what?" He didn't look down at the paper sitting on the mahogany table. His eyes were glued to my face, where they stayed without deviation. The only thing he seemed to care about was me. Not business. Not numbers.

"I'm buying you out. Stratosphere will be a Titan property."

He pushed the paper back without looking at it. "Forget business for a second."

"Business is the only commonality between us." I

slid the paper back toward him. "I have no interest in discussing anything else. I don't care for an explanation, an apology, or a justification. It is what it is, and I'd like to move forward."

"We aren't moving forward." He lowered his voice, his tone turning deadly. Every time I tried to control the situation, his aggression rose a few degrees. His magnetic field increased, affecting me and everything else in the building. He was a stronger opponent than all the others I'd faced. He got between my legs, made me fall in love with him like I didn't have a choice, and now he was still affecting me with his raw masculinity. I could smell testosterone in the air—because it was his cologne. "I didn't squeal to the *New York Times*, but I'm still trying to get sufficient proof for you. The reporter said the person called him on the phone. That's why he assumed it was me. I know that folder in my desk was incriminating. I don't blame you for assuming I betrayed you. I'd assume the same thing—"

"Then let it go. You got me. Good job." I finally raised my head and met his gaze, doing my best not to give the slightest reaction. I didn't show my rage or my heartbreak. Like I was speaking to a wall, I showed him the same indifference.

"Titan, it wasn't me. I had my PI get that information for me nearly two months ago. I admit I was going to read it. I wanted to know everything about you. I wanted to know why you were the way you were. But I didn't read it because I knew it was wrong. I respected you way too much to pry into your private life. When you were ready, I knew you would tell me. And that's what I did. I know that's hard to believe—"

"And I don't."

He sighed in agitation, like I was the one being difficult. "You have to believe me, Titan. Because if you don't, you're going to have a bigger problem on your hands. There's obviously someone out there who has it out for you. If they're framing me, then they know we're together. And if they know we're together, then there's another scandal coming your way. We have to figure out who it is—together."

When I listened to the sincerity in his voice, the obvious care in his tone, it made me want to believe him. My life would be so much easier if he were telling the truth. Being with Hunt was pure happiness. I'd never smiled so much. I'd never felt so at ease. Having that brutally taken away from me was just as bad as the actual betrayal. But all the evidence was stacked against him.

"You're the smartest woman I know. Why would I

do this? You're my business partner. When you look bad, I look bad."

"I'm your competition. So is Thorn."

"And you don't think marrying you fixes my problem?" he asked incredulously. "Once our assets are combined, I'll be launched to the very top of the list—as will you. It doesn't make any sense for me to betray you like this."

"You could get rid of Thorn."

"Again, once you're my wife, he'll bite the dust. Doesn't add up either."

"You've had it out for me since the beginning. You wanted to buy that publishing house from me."

"As an investment," he argued. "That was all. Nothing else."

This wouldn't go anywhere. He would just tell me more lies, and I would just ignore them. "I'm tired of talking about this—"

"Too damn bad. We're gonna talk about this until we figure it out." He slammed his hand on the table. "I'm not losing you, Titan. It's the first time in my life I actually feel like a whole person. I'm happy, and I'm not letting that go. I finally found a woman who makes me feel something, gives me a reason to work harder and be better. I'm not letting you go. And more importantly, there is someone out there that wants to hurt you. I can't let that happen. I need to protect you."

"I don't need your protection, Mr. Hunt—"

"Don't call me that." He leaned closer toward me, his eyes burning into mine. "I should have told you this sooner, but I kept forgetting in light of everything else going on in our lives. One night, I left your penthouse and saw Bruce Carol walk out. To my knowledge, I'm pretty sure he doesn't live there."

A lot of other successful businesspeople lived in Tribeca. It's possible he was visiting someone. "There's a lot more evidence against you than Bruce Carol right now."

"A month later, I saw him again. He got into a blacked-out car and drove off."

"What are you suggesting?"

"He's pissed at the way we destroyed him, and he's out to hurt both of us."

I held his expression while keeping my composure, but a tiny seed of doubt had been planted in the lining of my stomach. What scared me most was the fact that I wanted to trust Hunt even though the past taught me not to. Now, I didn't know what to think. Maybe Hunt hadn't seen Bruce Carol at all. Maybe he was just making that up to trick me. I didn't know what to think—and that scared me.

Hunt hardly blinked as he looked at me. "He could be watching us in your penthouse somehow. And now he's using all of this against us. It makes sense, Titan. It's the only thing that makes sense since I didn't do this. He's probably going to drop something else soon. He's probably going to tell everyone about us. We have to be prepared."

I couldn't listen to this anymore. His sweet words were getting into my heart. "If you told me the reporter got the information wrong, I might have believed you. I could go down there and hear him out. But the fact that the paperwork was in your drawer…"

He bowed his head and sighed.

"I just don't trust you. I don't trust anything you say. It sounds like a bunch of bullshit to me."

"Baby—"

"Don't ever call me that again."

He closed his eyes like I'd just backhanded him.

"I was a fool for letting you in. I was a fool for thinking a relationship with someone else would ever work. I'm done being made into a fool."

"I've never betrayed you. I've always had your back, Titan. I'm nothing but loyal."

"You need to figure out what loyalty means— because you obviously don't know." I grabbed the paper and pushed it back at him. "Now let's get this squared away so I never have to see you again."

The masculine sigh he exhaled was full of restrained rage. He turned his gaze to the paper where my offer was written in red ink. "No."

"That offer is already generous."

"There's no amount you could offer to make me sell." He ripped the page into pieces and tossed them onto the table. "The company has had no chance to grow. This place could easily be worth billions in a few years. I'm not selling a company that I believe in."

"Then name a price."

"I said there's no amount that will entice me." He straightened in his chair, his shoulders broad like a beam. It was one of my favorite features, the way he carried so much power in his body. When his arms were wrapped around me, I never felt safer. "We're staying partners, Titan."

"Then I'll sell."

"We both know that's not going to happen. I'm not giving you a dime. The only way you can walk away is if you leave empty-handed. And we know that's not going to happen after everything you invested."

So he was going to make this as difficult as possible.

"I'm not going anywhere. Neither are you. We're in this together."

This was the exact reason why I didn't go into business with anyone. I hated another person having power over me. They always abused it. I was tempted to walk away from this company, but I knew it would be a big success. And I didn't want to walk away from all the money I'd already invested into it. He was leaving me with no choice.

I pulled the paper away and presented the next one.

Hunt glanced at it, giving me a quizzical expression. "What is this?"

"Payment for your silence."

He eyed it again before he turned his furrowed eyebrows on me. "What the fuck is that supposed to mean?"

I pushed the NDA toward him. "Sign this, and you walk away with five million dollars." I could pay someone else a much smaller fee, but since Hunt was insanely wealthy, that was the smallest price that would entice him.

He didn't look at the paper again, staring at me like he hated me. He shook his head slightly, his jaw clenched.

"We never had a relationship. I don't have

arrangements. We're business associates, and that's all." I could live down this scandal in a few months. But if Hunt went public with this, it would ruin my reputation. The world would think I was a cheating freak.

He grabbed the pen off the table and added his signature.

I was relieved he signed it, but also hurt. All Hunt cared about was money. He probably sold my story to the newspaper because he was paid millions for it. If only he'd come to me first, I could have doubled the price.

After he added his signature, he crossed out the line in the contract that stated he would receive five million dollars. He scratched it out and wrote a zero on top. He pushed it back and slammed the pen down. "I don't want your money. I've never wanted your money. I just want you."

My hand trembled slightly, and I did my best to hide it.

His eyes were glued to mine. "I didn't sell your secret. And I would never sell any of your secrets." He pushed the paper back with a forceful shove. "It wasn't me, Titan. I'll say it as many times as it takes."

I placed the paper in my folder. "We're done here."

"Like hell, we are." His hand grabbed my wrist. He

squeezed it, but he didn't apply as much pressure as he usually did.

I couldn't let the touch linger. I couldn't let him play me—again. I yanked my hand away. "Don't ever touch me again, Hunt. If you do, I'll give you my signature right hook. And trust me, it hurts like hell." I left the table and walked away.

"Titan."

I kept walking.

"You know me, Titan. I would never do that to you. Just take some time to think about it."

I got to the door but didn't turn around.

"I'm not giving up on you."

My body wanted to freeze before I crossed the threshold, but I refused. When Hunt broke my heart, I gave up on love for good. It was over for me. I was grateful I had an arrangement that I could rely on. "I'm marrying Thorn."

"Over my dead body."

I looked at him over my shoulder, holding his gaze with steady eyes. "Then you're gonna die young."

# 3

HUNT

I DRANK A LOT THAT NIGHT.

My drink of choice? Old Fashioned.

My penthouse had never felt so empty. My life had never felt so lonely. I wasn't happy before Titan came along, and now that she was gone, I felt even worse than I had before. My bed wasn't comfortable anymore. Everything was heavy with the ghost she left behind. Her spirit haunted me. Her smile lived in my dreams.

I sat on the couch with her father's book on the sofa table. I'd read over half of it, getting to know a man I didn't have the honor of meeting. He mentioned Titan a few times, and I felt like I knew her as a young woman. She was more innocent then, unaffected by the evil in this world. She was pure and beautiful.

I missed her.

Brett called me, but I almost considered not answering. I wasn't in the mood to talk—only drink. But something compelled me to take the call. I answered. "Hmm?"

"I read the article about Titan...why did you leak it?"

"Fuck you."

"What?" he asked.

I rested the cool glass against my temple. "I didn't leak it."

"The reporter said you did."

"Well, I didn't," I snapped. "I would never do that to her...I love her."

Brett turned silent, probably because he'd never heard me say that about her. He'd never heard me say that about anyone. "Are you drinking?"

"What else would I be doing?"

"I'm down the road. I'm gonna come by."

"Why?"

"Because you sound like shit." Click.

I tossed the phone on the table and poured another drink. The amber liquid reminded me of her dark hair. I missed fisting it every night. I missed making love to her without a condom. I'd never been with a woman without latex wrapped around my dick. We had an experience I'd never enjoyed with anyone else. She was special to me in so many ways. I admired the beauty behind those bright eyes. I admired her for her courage, her strength, not all the money in her bank account. I loved this woman with all my heart.

Brett walked inside ten minutes later. I was so drunk I had no grasp of time. It seemed like only a few seconds had passed. He helped himself to my kitchen and got a glass of water before he came back. He snatched the liquor out of my hand and downed it himself.

"Get your own."

"I'm cutting you off." He grabbed the bottle of whiskey and tucked it into his side on the couch. "You turn into an ass when you drink."

"I thought I was already an ass."

"Well, you are. But you turn into a bigger ass."

I drank the water just so I had something to do with my hands.

"So, you didn't go to the newspaper?"

"Fuck no. Like I would ever do that."

"Then what happened?"

I told him the story, up until my recent conversation with Titan at Stratosphere.

"You really think someone is framing you?"

"What other explanation is there? They impersonated me to the reporter. He wanted me to take the fall."

"And Bruce Carol is the only person you can think of?"

"Yeah."

"Shit." He rubbed the back of his head. "And she really thinks you did it?"

"Yes. But she would have believed me if she hadn't found those papers in the bottom of my desk. Why didn't I throw those away?"

"You really didn't read them?"

"No. I realized it was a jackass thing to do, so I stopped myself. I respect that woman like a queen. I would never do anything to hurt her in the slightest. I know she knows that...deep down inside. She's been hurt, and I understand why she's afraid to listen to me. She's been through a lot, and it's already hard for her to trust people. She puts on a brave face for me, but I know she's devastated... I know how much I hurt her." I dragged my hand down my face, overwhelmed with misery.

"But you didn't hurt her, Hunt. Someone else did it —not you."

"She doesn't know that, Brett. She thinks I never really loved her...that I was just using her."

"Then we have to figure out a way to prove it to her."

"How?" I demanded. "I could have my PI follow

Bruce Carol around, but what good will that do? The damage is already done."

Brett sank into the couch and looked at the TV. It was on, but the volume was low. The blue and yellow glow from the screen bounced off the walls of the living room. He stared at it for a long time, wearing the same expression I wore when I was seriously considering something.

All I'd been doing was thinking about how to fix this. If only those papers had been thrown away, Titan would still be mine. She would have listened to me. I know she would have. Why did I have to be such an idiot?

"There's one thing I can think of…"

"I'm desperate, Brett. Tell me."

"You aren't going to like it."

"Shut up and tell me."

He could have made a smartass remark in return, but he didn't. "The best way to bury a story is to get everyone talking about something else."

"Okay." How did that help me?

"If you give the media something else to print, then no one will care about Titan's story. It'll fade into the background."

"Well, I don't have any other stories."

"That's not true."

"I'm drunk, Brett. Be clearer."

"Everyone wants to know what happened between you and your father. Reporters have pestered both you and Vincent about it, and neither one of you have talked."

"For a reason."

"If you gave them the full story, people wouldn't shut up about it. It would make the front page of every newspaper and magazine. It would be on every news station. Nobody would give a damn about the abusive boyfriend Titan had ten years ago. All the attention would be on you, not her."

I rested the back of my neck on the edge of the couch and stared at the ceiling. "My father and I already hate each other. He's pissed at me over Megaland. I don't want to stir the pot."

"I said you wouldn't like it."

I sighed into the room.

"Not only would it get everyone talking about something else, but Titan would have to acknowledge your own actions. You'd basically be falling on your sword, sacrificing yourself for her. It might make her believe your innocence. And if not, she would at least think you were sorry for what you did."

That was tempting.

"Or you could prove you were framed. But like you said, that could be impossible."

I ran my fingers through my hair, wishing it was Titan who was touching me. "If I do this, I'd basically declare war on my father."

"It's not like you're on great terms anyway."

"But he'll think I'm provoking him."

"Maybe you should give him a heads-up."

I shook my head. "I'm not speaking to him ever again."

"Then I'm out of options. That's all I can think of."

I didn't throw Titan under the bus to begin with, so it wasn't fair for me to sacrifice myself to distract the rest of the herd. But I had to get this woman back—at any cost. Just like water, air, and food, I couldn't live without her.

I'd die without her.

# 4

TITAN

THORN and I sat in the back seat of the car while my driver took me to the news station. I agreed to do an interview with the biggest broadcasting company in the nation. My story was getting more attention with every passing day, and if I didn't make a statement, it would seem like I was hiding something.

Thorn grabbed my hand and held it on his thigh. "You've got this, Titan."

"I know."

"Did you see the statement I made to the *New Yorker*?"

I shook my head.

He grabbed his phone and showed me the quote.

WHEN WE ASKED THORN CUTLER ABOUT THE NEWS OF

his girlfriend, Tatum Titan, he only had a short statement to make. "Ms. Titan has endured a lot in her past, but it doesn't define who she's become. I think this will only make the world admire her even more than they already did. I know I do."

My eyes met his, and I smiled. "Thanks, Thorn."

"Of course. This interview will get the world on your side. I know it will."

"I hope you're right. I don't want their judgment, their pity."

We pulled up to the station then walked inside. I was doing a live interview in just thirty minutes. I walked into the studio and took a seat in front of a mirror, knowing they would do my makeup first.

"Ms. Titan." Olivia James walked up to me, her makeup done and her hair perfectly styled. She was ready for the cameras. "I'm so sorry to do this, but the interview has been canceled. A news story has just been dropped, and we have to spend our hour covering it."

"What news story?" Thorn asked.

"Diesel Hunt," she said. "He just gave the biggest interview of the year."

SIDE BY SIDE IN THE BACK SEAT OF THE CAR, WE watched on Thorn's phone.

Diesel wore a black suit with a matching tie. It fit his muscular body perfectly, and his coffee eyes were piercing more than usual. He sat across from the interviewer, calm and collected like he was sitting in a meeting. He was so handsome it was unnerving. He looked like a man who should be in film, not business.

John Bettencourt sat across from him, his list of questions written on his card. "The last time you and your father were photographed together was nearly ten years ago. Have you spoken since that moment?" He got right into the interview.

"Is he going to talk about his father?" I asked incredulously.

"Looks like it," Thorn said. "But why? What does he get out of this?"

Hunt's expression didn't change as he took the question. "Shortly after that photo was taken. My father is an astute businessman. He taught me everything I know. I would be lying if I said he hasn't had a tremendous impact on my life."

"But you haven't spoken since?"

Hunt shook his head slightly before he answered. "No."

"Why is that?"

Hunt didn't fidget in his chair, but he didn't rush into the answer. He wore a black watch, and he held himself like he was the one conducting the interview. The topic made him uncomfortable, but he never showed it. "We disagreed on a lot of things."

"Money?"

"No."

"Then what?" John pressed.

"My mother had a son before she met my father. When she passed away, my father took him in. But he never loved him. My younger brother Jax and I were always treated differently. We went to the best schools, had the best clothes...but my eldest brother was outcast. When it came to a point where I couldn't take it anymore, I left. My father made me choose—and I chose my brother."

"Oh my god..." I covered my mouth as I watched Hunt confess the truth to the entire world.

John asked Hunt to reflect on his childhood memories and his mother, but I stopped listening.

"I can't believe he did that." I didn't see any advantage to telling the world about his painful relationship with his father. It was bound to piss off Vincent Hunt, and they were already butting heads.

"I can't believe he did that either. There's only one explanation for it."

"What?" I asked.

"He's trying to take the focus off you."

———

THE REPORTERS DISAPPEARED FROM OUTSIDE MY building. Not a single one lingered behind. I walked into my building without a single camera pointed in my face and took the elevator to my penthouse.

It was nice to be home.

I made myself a drink and sat on the couch. My stilettos were kicked off, and I let my feet relax.

All I could think about was Hunt and that interview.

My phone went off with a text message. *You must have seen my interview by now*. It was Hunt.

I stared at the screen, unsure what to say.

*I'm in the lobby of your building.*

Of course he was. Why didn't that surprise me? I checked the code to my elevator, but I was certain Hunt wouldn't try to come up without being invited.

But if he knew I was home, that meant he saw me walk inside. He wasn't far behind me.

*Titan.*

He knew I was staring at the phone right that second. He could read me without even being in the room with me. I should tell him to leave me alone, but I wanted to talk to him. I wanted to ask him about that interview...ask if he was okay. I shouldn't care, but of course, I did.

I walked to the elevator and hit the code so the doors would open.

When he didn't text again, I knew he'd stepped inside. The light over the elevator lit up as it counted the floors. It beeped before the doors opened, and I came face-to-face with the same Hunt I saw on TV. He was even in the same suit.

I crossed my arms over my chest and forced myself not to take a breath, not to let my body react to him naturally. Each time he walked into the room, I was a little weaker than I was before. My mouth ached for his. My body did too.

But those days were over.

He stepped inside with his eyes fixed on me, that intensity burning holes in my skin. He still looked at me like he owned me, like I was his possession. He closed in on me and barely left any space between us.

He smelled exactly the same.

I looked up into his face, maintaining the stoic expression I wore around people I didn't trust.

Because I didn't trust him anymore.

I was the first one to speak. "Are you okay?"

He tilted his head slightly as he looked at my mouth. The heat radiated off him, the desire to press his mouth to mine. But he didn't move in because I would only pull away. His eyes took in the rest of my features, slowly drinking them in like he hadn't seen me in years. "You know I'm not okay."

I knew he wasn't referring to the interview. He was referring to the distance between us, to the end of the most beautiful relationship I'd ever known. It was full of passion, trust, love...and now it was gone. "Why did you do it?"

"You're a smart woman, Titan. You'll figure it out."

"You did it so people would stop talking about me..."

His only response was a slight nod.

"Why, Hunt? Why do you care?"

"You're the woman I love," he whispered. "Of course I care."

My heart ached with a pain that wouldn't subside. I was livid with him, I didn't trust him, but I loved him —so goddamn much.

"My father is pissed. He's probably smashed everything in his house by now. I'll pay for the interview...in many ways. But no one cares about your story anymore, Titan. It's old news, and it won't surface again. Everyone will be talking about this for months...if not years. You still believe I betrayed you?"

I stared at his hard jaw, the smooth skin that was cleanly shaven. I used to run my lips over that chiseled jawline. I used to plant kisses there when he was asleep beside me. Now I stared at it because I couldn't meet his gaze.

"Why would I sabotage myself for you?" he whispered. "Why would I make this sacrifice if I'd really stabbed you in the back?"

"I don't know..."

"Because there is no reason. I've always been loyal to you. I just proved it."

His scent was overwhelming, and the look in his eyes burned me. I stepped back, needing the space to breathe.

But he crowded me once again. "I'm not going away, Titan. If I'd betrayed you, I would admit it. But I never did."

"The papers were in your drawer..."

"But I never read them. And I certainly didn't show them to anyone."

I looked at the ground because I couldn't stand the intensity in those brown eyes. "I don't know what to think."

His hand moved to my chin, forcing me to look at him. "Yes, you do. Maybe all the evidence says I'm guilty. But you know I'm not."

I enjoyed the touch of his hand so much. I nearly closed my eyes when he felt me. A moan almost escaped my lips. But the terror gripped me by the throat. I had no idea if he was guilty or innocent, and that made me afraid. I stepped back so his touch would disappear. "Maybe you did tell that reporter, but it was a month ago. You fell in love with me in the meantime, and now that the story is out, you needed to do something to win me back."

"No."

"Maybe you did want the world to know because you thought it would break me. Then you could take Stratosphere all for yourself."

He shook his head slightly. "I fell in love with you because you're unbreakable. It's gonna take something a lot stronger than this story to chip away at you. My woman doesn't bend. She doesn't break. Not for anyone, not for me."

It was painfully sweet, smooth all the way down.

"Maybe you regret what you did, and you're just trying to make up for it."

"No. The only reason why I did it was to prove my loyalty to you. If I had done it, I just erased all its effectiveness. I threw my reputation, my own family, under the bus. We both know that doesn't add up."

I took another step back, hardly able to breathe.

"Baby."

"Don't call me that—"

"Baby." His hands moved into my hair, and he crowded me, his body moving into mine. He pressed his forehead to mine and held me there, touching me, existing with me. "I know you're scared. I know you're hurt. But I swear on my mother's grave, it wasn't me. I'm a man who will always admit his faults. I'll always be honest with you. If I made a mistake, I would say it. But I didn't do this."

My hands moved to his wrists, and I felt his steady heartbeat. I felt the prominent veins that were corded within his skin. I felt the tight muscle, the subtle shift every time he moved. I felt the heat that burned on the surface of his body. I closed my eyes, savoring the touch of this man.

Then he kissed me. Softly and sensually, his mouth moved against mine.

I kissed him back, my mind turned off and my

body taking control. My tongue greeted his, and my mouth was flooded with his warm breath. I wanted to be loved by this man for the night. I wanted to be loved by this man all my life.

But I couldn't.

I stepped back and ended the wet kiss. "Hunt, you should go."

"No."

"Don't make this harder than it needs to be."

The dark sexiness in his eyes disappeared as a shadow passed. His anger turned to fury, his fury to rage. "Titan, you're better than this. Think it through. Don't push me away when I belong right beside you. Don't let them win."

"I need to think about it."

"No, you don't."

"Yes. I do." I took another step back even though he wasn't crowding me. He didn't try to rush me again. He kept his distance this time, his anger keeping him back. "I understand everything that you said. I understand everything that's happened. But this is complicated and doesn't deserve a simple answer. Outside of Thorn and me, you were the only one who knew about what happened."

"But—"

"Trust is the hardest thing for me to give. It comes

naturally for most people, but for me, it's like giving up my heart. I gave you my trust so quickly because it felt right. You stood up for me when other men wouldn't. You admired me when most men would call me bossy. You swept me off my feet instantly. And that's where everything went wrong...it happened too fast."

"It didn't happen fast enough, if you ask me." His powerful arms hung by his sides, tense in the jacket that hugged his body. He showed a tense jaw, furrowed eyebrows. He was angry, but dangerously sexy at the same time.

"I don't know you, Diesel Hunt."

"Yes, you do."

"I've known you for a few months. I've known Thorn for a decade."

"Irrelevant."

"I shouldn't have trusted you so quickly. Now that this has happened, I can't trust you again."

"I. Didn't. Do. It."

"There's no way for me to know. You're doing and saying all the right things, but will I ever really know? I'm not a risk-taker. You know that. All the risks I've taken have cost me more than I bet in the first place. I learned my lesson the first time...and now I learned it again."

"Don't compare me to him."

"That's not how I meant it—"

"It sounded like it."

"Bottom line is...I don't trust you." I looked him in the eye as I said, knowing he needed to understand I meant it. There was no explanation for how my past was leaked. Hunt had one story along with his own theories, but I couldn't prove any of them. Unless the proof was right in front of me, it was unknown. "That's not going to change. Everything is different. It's too risky."

"Baby—"

"I'm not going to change my mind, Hunt. I was scared to begin with, but now I'm too scared to give this another try. I'm afraid it'll ruin everything I've worked so hard for. Thorn is safe. There's no one in the world I trust more."

His chest rose and fell at a quicker rate, the rage obvious in his eyes.

"You should go."

He didn't move. Like a mountain, he stood absolutely still and weathered the storm. His feet were firmly planted on the ground.

I crossed my arms over my chest and hugged myself, feeling the shot of pain all over again. The betrayal happened again in my mind, the raw cut that caused an open wound. I was still bleeding everywhere because I hadn't had time to deal. It would be a scar eventually, the kind of scar everyone could see. "I don't think we should do business together anymore, but if you leave me no choice..."

"I'm not going anywhere."

"Hunt, nothing is going to change. We will only be business partners from now on..."

He gave me a hard stare.

I refused to say anything else, making my statement clear. Bringing the attention on to himself was touching. I'd have to be made of stone not to appreciate it. But it didn't change the circumstance. Too much had changed. I didn't feel the same way anymore. If I were to be with him again, I would constantly be paranoid. That wasn't how a relationship should be. With Thorn, I would get everything I wanted—without heartbreak. "Please go, Hunt."

He stayed rooted to the spot, the anger in his eyes changing to obvious disappointment. The burn in his expression fading to a painful stare. He slid his hands into his pockets, and he finally took a step back.

It hurt to watch him walk away.

He turned around, hit the button, and then stepped into the elevator.

He stared at me as the doors closed. They inched

to the center until he was completely blocked from view. The elevator beeped before it began to descend.

I didn't cry over anything. Crying was a waste of time and a waste of energy. But the tears built up in my eyes on their own, becoming thicker and heavier. My vision blurred, and I felt them streak down my cheeks. The last time I cried, I'd told Hunt I loved him.

And now I cried again when I told him goodbye.

# 5

HUNT

I was the kind of man who never gave up.

If I wanted something, I didn't stop until I got it.

That applied to business, to tasks.

Never people.

I'd never wanted a woman that I couldn't have. Women wanted to get into my pants because I had a reputation for bringing the heat to the sheets. Or they wanted to be close to my wallet, to take a ride in my Bugatti. They wanted to know how I became so successful, like I'd part with my secrets if they sucked my cock well enough.

But they never cared about me.

Tatum Titan didn't need a damn thing from me. There wasn't anything I could give her that she couldn't give herself. The only thing she wanted from me...was me. She actually cared about me. She loved me for everything underneath my designer suits, for my flesh and bone.

And now she was gone.

I'd put myself on the line when I told the world about my father. Now I was being hit with questions left and right, questions I didn't want to answer. I'd tarnished my father's reputation with a past he wanted to stay buried. I'd basically declared war on him.

For one woman.

But it didn't matter. It didn't win back her trust. It didn't win back her heart.

It was all for nothing.

I shouldn't have been surprised by her decision. It took so long for her to open up to me in the first place. For months, we got to know each other over sex and limited conversation. It took months for her just to crack her shell. Even then, she hid most of herself behind her eyes. She kept her walls tall and thick.

But over time, I slowly knocked them down.

I defeated all of her walls until I was deep inside her, seeing her bare soul when no one could. I had her under my thumb, had her right next to my heart. I got past Tatum Titan and finally got to just Tatum…the beautiful woman at her core.

But then she was taken from me.

It didn't surprise me that she ran off. It didn't

surprise me that she wouldn't give me another chance. She stuck out her neck for me and got the edge of a blade. She got too close to the fire then got burned. She wasn't the kind of woman who ever took risks because her past taught her not to.

And now she was too terrified ever to trust me again.

Unless I cleared my name beyond a reasonable doubt, she would never be mine again.

Fuck.

I spent the next few days camped out in my penthouse. Unknown numbers kept calling me, I was all over the news, and my inbox was flooded with prying emails. All the heat was on me. Not a single person was thinking about Titan anymore.

When I'd pictured myself moving on with my life, I didn't know what direction I should take. Before I met Titan, my life was pretty simple—but also mundane. I went out to the clubs with friends, picked up a few women, and fucked late into the night. I had business meetings during the week. I counted my checks and dropped them off at the bank. I had so much, but I felt so empty at the same time. Good sex was easy to come by, but great sex like I had with Titan was unheard of.

That woman invigorated me.

Could I go back to before? Now that I'd known something so much better?

The idea of kissing another woman didn't arouse me at all. She could be a supermodel, and that wouldn't make a difference. I didn't want to bury myself between a woman's legs with a condom wrapped around my length. There was only one person I wanted to be with, only one fantasy I wanted to have.

I was a one-woman man now.

I knew Titan better than anyone, and when she said she wouldn't change her mind, she meant it. There was nothing I could offer her to alter that. She was scared of me, didn't trust me.

So now I was stuck. I didn't want to move on from this woman, but this woman didn't want me.

There was never a problem I couldn't solve. But this problem didn't have a solution.

None that I could see.

———

I DIDN'T CARE THAT MUCH ABOUT STRATOSPHERE. IT was a viable company with a lot of potential. One day, it would be one of the biggest companies in the world. With Titan's vision and my experience, we would turn it into a household name. But I was already wealthy and had other companies to invest my time in.

Titan was the only reason I was still there.

It was the only connection I had to her. Even if I couldn't have her the way I used to, I needed to have some of her. She was important to my happiness. I'd rather have some of her than none of her at all.

I stepped out of the elevator and greeted my assistants. I had a few messages along with some mail. I took everything and glanced at Titan's office.

The door was open.

I set my paperwork on my desk then walked across the floor to her office. My heart was beating hard in my chest as the adrenaline coursed through my veins. This woman got my heart pumping like no one else. I suspected she would always have this effect on me, even if she came to work with her son on her arm. She could have a family with Thorn, and I would still desire her the same way.

I tapped my knuckles against the open door.

She was sitting at her desk with perfect posture, her slender fingertips hitting the keyboard at a quick speed. During working hours, she hustled to get things done. There were only so many hours in a day, and she spent her time wisely. She wore a tight black dress with a silver necklace around her throat. Her hair was pulled back into a sleek ponytail, showing her beautiful face and the prominent cheekbones that led to smoky eyes. She could hit the runway with a group of models and fit right in.

She looked up when she realized I was at the door. But her look was void of any kind of reaction. She must have suspected it was me, that we couldn't avoid each other forever. I'd stayed away for a few days so we both could recover from the painful conversation we'd had.

Although neither one of us would ever really recover from it.

"Hello, Mr. Hunt." She spoke to me like I was some business associate that she could barely remember. She had to force herself to remember my name because it was too insignificant to commit to memory.

Like a sore muscle that wouldn't heal, the title was a dull pain. I was used to her calling me by my first name, the name that no one else ever addressed me as. She had a right that no one else had ever attained. It was personal, intimate, because that was how our relationship had been. "Call me Hunt." If I asked her to call me Diesel, she wouldn't do it. But the Mr. part was just annoying.

She gave a slight nod but no other reaction. "Something you need?"

My eyes were locked on her face, her red-painted lips. The last time I kissed that mouth, she tasted like salty watermelon. Kissing her felt like the most natural thing in the world. It brought silence to a chaotic world, it brought peace into my constantly shifting mind. I took a seat in one of the armchairs facing her desk and rested my ankle on the opposite knee. "I've been thinking about the image of the company lately." I didn't need to explain exactly what that meant. She'd been scrutinized over her past relationship with Jeremy, and I was being fried for my family problems. We were both taking a lot of heat. "We need to do something to rectify it, some good publicity. I just took a look at the stocks—"

"I saw them too."

"We need to do something. I've been getting a lot of attention, but it's not necessarily good attention. Even though my father was an ass, people still condemn me for turning my back on him. We should make an appearance together. It doesn't have to be a personal one, but something that shows strength and unity. People will respond to that."

"I think you might be right."

"There's the annual Business Expo in Cannes, France next week. We should make a presentation there. We'll both be able to get out of the country, and people will start to forget about us since we're focused on work. We can talk about Stratosphere and the improvements we have in store. We can unveil all our new products, and the world will be talking about that —instead of us."

She nodded. "I think that's a good idea. I love Cannes anyway."

"As do I." It was a beautiful city with great views of the French Riviera. The water was so blue, so deep. It reminded me of the Virgin Islands. "I'll make the arrangements. In the meantime, we need to work on the presentation. I can have a team put something together, but I'm sure you like the hands-on approach."

"I do."

"Then let me know a time that works best for you."

"I can do it on my own, Hunt." She was avoiding me at all costs, doing everything she could to stay away from me.

There was no way out of this. "Titan."

Her eyes remained focused on mine. She hid her unease, her trepidation. When I stared at her like that, she usually yielded to me. But now that our romance was over, she wouldn't bend again. She wouldn't submit the way she used to.

"We're partners. That's never going to change. This

company is going to be exceptional because we're exceptional. We have to work together. We do everything together—not separately. I can be professional if you give me that same respect."

This time, she couldn't control her reaction. The hardness of her eyes melted away. My words brought her relief but also sadness. "That's fair."

"Let me know what time works best for you." I rose from the chair and buttoned the front of my suit. I knew her desire for me didn't change. When she kissed me, all those feelings were still there. She wanted to grip my broad shoulders and ride me slowly on the couch, like we'd done dozens of times before. I wanted to take her on her desk right then and there, her dress pulled up to her waist and her panties pushed to the side.

But I kept walking, knowing she was staring at my ass the second I turned around.

Her quiet voice sounded from behind me. "I will."

---

MUSIC.

Dim lights.

Alcohol.

Women.

Silhouettes.

I was back in time. I was in a prime booth in one of the hottest nightclubs in Manhattan. There was a line out the door and around the block, but I walked inside without even having to give my name. Pine and Mike were doing shots off women's bodies, having the time of their lives.

I was the center of all of it, but my mind was somewhere else. A blonde took the seat beside me, rubbed my thigh with her long fingertips, and did her best to flirt with me. Her touch wasn't arousing. Titan was forward, but she was never desperate. She was classy in everything she did, even when it came to sex.

Pine pulled up a woman's dress and revealed her tight stomach. He did a shot then licked the salt right off her body.

She threw her arms up. "Woo!"

He pulled her into his lap and stuck his tongue down her throat, her panties still on display for everyone to see.

I looked away, my thoughts returning to Titan even though they never left.

The blonde at my side took advantage of the way I turned my head and kissed me on the mouth. Just like Pine did, she went for the kill right away. She gave her tongue and desperately tried to take mine.

I didn't feel a damn thing.

Just repulsed.

I turned my face away, rejecting her without sparing her feelings. "I have to go." I pulled out my wallet and threw some cash on the table to cover all the drinks we'd ordered. Then I moved through the crowd of dark bodies and made it back to the entrance. The cool night air hit me and cleansed me of the muggy smell of alcohol and perfume. It was a beautiful night in Manhattan, but I didn't enjoy it. I just wanted to have a quiet dinner with one woman, make love, and then go to sleep.

But that was too much to ask for.

"Hunt, what the hell?" Pine came up from behind me.

I was surprised he'd noticed I left. "What's up?" I turned to him with my hands in my pockets. My Bullet was parked right along the curb, and I was eager to get it on the road. People were crowding next to it so they could get a closer look.

"What's up?" he asked. "You just take off without saying goodbye?"

"I have business to take care of. And you looked occupied."

"She can wait." He waved her off like she was standing right there. "Are you sure you're alright?"

I didn't talk about my feelings with my crew. As far as I was concerned, none of us had feelings. "I'm fine, man. Go back inside and enjoy your night."

"You haven't been the same in a long time. And now this stuff with your dad...you seem low."

"I am low." I never told him about Titan because she asked me not to. I still kept her secret even though nothing was forcing me to do it. I signed an NDA, but I wasn't scared of the legal ramifications.

"Let's get a drink at my place," he said. "We can talk about it."

I didn't want to talk. I didn't want to think. I didn't want anything. I clapped him on the shoulder, touched by the offer. "I appreciate that, man. But I'm really okay. Go back inside and do some more shots."

Pine continued to eye me.

The blonde from inside walked out and spotted me. Her eyes were heavy, and she was obviously drunk. Maybe she needed to be wasted to have the courage to kiss me. She had tasted like booze. She wobbled as she walked up to me. "Hunt..."

I grabbed her by the arm so she wouldn't topple over. "I'm gonna take her home. You go inside, Pine."

"Are you sure?" he asked.

"Absolutely." I moved my arm around her waist and guided her to my car.

"Oh my god! The Bullet..."

"Yeah." I opened the passenger door. "Just don't puke in it, alright?"

"Okay..."

Once she was buckled in, I took her to her apartment then headed back to my place. I spent my evening with a bottle of scotch and my thoughts for company.

I WAS SITTING in the conference room waiting for Hunt when Thorn texted me.

*Thought you'd want to know.* He attached a link to the message.

The headline popped up before I clicked on it. *Diesel Hunt's Night on the Town.* It opened to a short article with pictures. I didn't need to read the words to deduce what the story was about. There was a picture of him kissing a blonde in a booth. He was photographed with the same woman as they got into his Bullet.

I felt like someone stabbed me.

The image was burned into my brain, and now I couldn't shake it off. So much nausea overcame me that I nearly threw up on the table. I closed the article because I couldn't look at it anymore. I didn't want to think about his lips on anyone. I didn't want to think about what they did when they got back to his place.

I felt stupid for ever thinking he might be telling the truth.

He was back to fucking every woman in Manhattan.

I didn't matter to him. He never loved me. He only used me.

I didn't notice him walk in behind me because my thoughts had been glued to those images. My first instinct was to storm off and leave, to throw my tablet at his head and tell him to fuck off. But he was free to do whatever he wanted. We weren't together anymore. Now we were just business partners, and I had to be professional with him even if I despised him.

"Morning." He moved to the seat across from me and set his things on the surface of the table.

I had to swallow my rage. I had to control my temper. I had to keep calm. If I let my fury rise, he would win. He would know he hurt me. Indifference was my only defense.

When I didn't say it back, he met my gaze.

It took all my strength to say it back. "Morning."

He opened his folder and placed his phone on the

table. "She kissed me, and I turned away. That photo is misleading."

My eyebrows jumped up my forehead, and my heart squeezed all the blood back into my veins. My blood pressure dropped, and I felt weak for several seconds, caught off guard by his intuition. How did he know I knew about it? How did he know I was upset? Did he figure it out just by looking at me? Was he able to read all my masks?

"I took her home because I was leaving and she was drunk off her ass. She could barely walk. I drove her to her apartment then went home. Nothing happened."

All I felt was relief when I shouldn't feel anything at all. But I was also plagued with suspicion. He could be feeding me lines right that second. The picture was pretty incriminating. But I also understood how the media could turn everything upside down. "Why are you telling me this?"

"Because I know you're devastated."

I tried to harden my expression, but it was already at full capacity. I couldn't appear more indifferent, more cold, if I tried. My shield was up, but it did nothing to deflect his intimate blows. "I couldn't care less, Hunt." I sounded convincing to my ears, but that might not be enough.

"Really?" he asked. "Because I'd be devastated if I saw you kiss someone."

Now I was right back to where I was in the beginning. I was touched by his words, touched by his jealousy. I had been heartbroken when I looked at that picture. We were no longer together, but the idea of him just touching someone made me sick to my stomach. I was still possessive of him even when he wasn't mine. "I have no reason to believe you."

"Why would I lie?" He stared me down with his brooding gaze. "If I fucked someone, I would tell you. If I'm really lying about everything, then you should be scared. Because I would have a serious personality disorder."

I didn't have an argument against that because he was right. He would have to be a psychopath to act like one person then completely flip on me. Even now, it was hard to believe he would do those things to me. Evidence was staring at me right in the face, and I still wanted to believe him. "Why do you care what I think?"

He leaned back in his chair, his crisp suit fitting that muscular body perfectly. His hair was starting to come in again on his chin, and his brown eyes looked warm on this cool afternoon. He was so gorgeous it hurt sometimes. It made me want to forget everything that happened and jump into his bed right then and there. "Because I'm still loyal to you, Titan. I don't want you to think I'm fucking someone else when the only person I want to fuck is you."

---

THE ELEVATOR DOOR OPENED, AND THORN WALKED inside with a bag of takeout. "Thought you might be hungry."

"I have no appetite."

"And that's exactly why I'm here." He set the bag on the dining table and pulled out two chicken dinners from the French restaurant just down the street. "I know you haven't been eating...at least, more than usual."

I was too sick to eat anything. I was too heart-broken to feel a different sensation besides pain. The only craving I had was for strong whiskey with a hint of orange and cherry.

"Sit, Titan."

I joined him at the table with my Old Fashioned.

He swapped that out with two glasses of water. "I'm cutting you off."

"I'm not drunk, Thorn."

"Are you kidding me?" he asked. "You're

always drunk. You just hide it better than everyone else." He grabbed his fork and dug in. "By the way, I'm not leaving until you eat all of that." He'd ditched his suit and tie for dark jeans and a t-shirt. His ripped arms filled out the material perfectly. With light blond hair and bright eyes, he was a pretty man. Our children would be beautiful.

But my children with Hunt would have been gorgeous.

Fighting Thorn would be a losing battle, and I knew he was right. I needed to eat. I wasn't getting enough calories, and I was malnourished. Being weak wouldn't do me any favors. I picked up the fork and ate.

We enjoyed the companionable silence together.

"How are you?" he finally asked.

"I'm okay. Hunt and I are going to Cannes in a few days...for a business conference."

"Are you okay with that?"

"I'll be fine."

"You want me to come along?"

"No." I had to deal with Hunt every day. There was no way to avoid it. "What's new with you?"

"My mom has been worried about you. When that story hit the papers...she was really upset. She asked if she should call you or send you flowers. I told her to leave you alone for a while."

"She's so sweet…"

"She doesn't think less of you. I think she likes you even more, Titan."

"She'll be a great mother-in-law. I'm very lucky."

Thorn stopped eating to look at me. "Does that mean you want to marry me again?"

I nodded. "If you'll have me. I understand if your answer has changed."

"Of course, it hasn't. I just wasn't sure how you felt about it."

"No. I shouldn't have changed my mind to begin with. It was stupid to ever think marrying Hunt was a good idea. I haven't even known him that long…it's only been a few months. It was naïve of me to think he was the right person."

"You're being hard on yourself. I liked him too… once upon a time."

"I still jumped the gun."

"You fell in love, Titan. It happens to the best of us. Don't beat yourself up over it."

I stared at my food. "You're so good to me."

"You know I always have your back, Titan. You can't count on anyone else in the world, but you can always count on me."

And that was exactly why I was marrying him. I was never afraid of a betrayal from him, of a lie. He was like family to me, someone I could count on no matter what. My relationship with Hunt never compared to that. "I know…"

Thorn eyed me for a moment before he turned his attention back to his food. "I know that picture of Hunt must have hurt you… You can talk about it if you want."

"He told me he turned away when that woman kissed him…the picture was misleading. And then he took her home afterward. Nothing happened."

"And you believe him?"

"I…I don't know." I dropped my fork and covered my face with my hands. "When he says these things, I want to believe him. A part of me actually does believe him. I think he didn't sell me out to reporters…that he really didn't read those papers his PI got him. Now I think he didn't hook up with some blonde in a club. Is that stupid?"

Thorn stared at me, not giving an answer.

I dragged my hands down my face then set them on the table. "It is stupid, isn't it?"

He continued his silence.

"Thorn, what do you think?"

"What I think doesn't matter."

"Yes, it does. I want to know."

He sighed before he answered. "You know him better than I do...but I think he's lying about everything. There's no way he had those papers sitting in his drawer unless he was going to do something with them. If he hadn't read them, he would have destroyed them and got rid of the evidence. But he probably made copies and gave them to the reporter and kept a copy for himself just in case he needed them. His office is safer than his home, so that would explain why he left them there. He was caught on camera kissing that woman in the club. If that's not evidence, I don't know what it is."

My heart sank further and further. "He signed that NDA and didn't accept the money I offered. Why would he do that?"

"To throw you off his scent."

"To what end?" I asked. "He knows I'll never trust him again."

"I don't know. Maybe he wants your expertise to grow the company. When it's worth billions, he'll squeeze you out by threatening to go public."

"But why reveal my past to the reporters to begin with?" I argued.

"Why would the *New York Times* name him as the source if they weren't sure it was him?"

Every question I had was met with a dead end. Hunt looked guilty every time—as much as I wanted to believe he was innocent.

"I know this is hard because you love him, but…it's just how it is."

Why was this happening to me? Why couldn't I just fall in love like everyone else? Why couldn't I fall for the right man? Why couldn't I love Thorn and have him love me back? That would be the simplest solution.

Thorn eyed me with obvious pity. "People are greedy and evil. They'll use you until they get what they want. And once they have it, they'll forget about you. It's why I've never fallen in love. It's why I'll never fall in love."

"Thorn, you know that's not true."

"Yes, it is."

I looked at his hard blue eyes and saw a little softness in them, something only I could see because I knew where to look. "What about us? We're nothing like that."

"We're one of the few, and we're very lucky that we found each other."

I hated to imagine my life without him. Thorn was the family I needed when I lost my own. He helped me get through the pain, helped me become the strong woman I was now. He was the only man in my life I could truly rely on. He would take care of me no matter what. I could afford to buy anything in the world, but there was no amount of money that could buy loyalty. "Yeah, you're right."

He tapped his fingers against the wood. "I meant what I said. I'm not leaving until you eat all of that."

I grabbed my fork again and stirred the food around. "I know, Thorn. And thanks for making me eat it."

"One day, I'll be as low as you are now. And it'll be your turn to make me eat."

I gave a halfhearted smile. "You have yourself a deal."

He finished his food long before I did and looked out the window as I finished. His jaw was free of hair because he shaved every morning. Sometimes Hunt let his hair grow out, but Thorn never did. He had a distinctive clean look, fair skin with bright eyes. He couldn't be more different from Hunt. They were both handsome men, just in different shades.

I should let Hunt go, but it was hard for me to walk away. "I guess I want to believe him because of the way he looks at me..."

Thorn turned his gaze on me.

"He just...looks at me like he loves me. Like I'm the

only thing in the world that matters. That look has never changed, even now. I know everything that's happened has contradicted that...but that's how I feel."

Thorn bowed his head slightly as he stared at the table instead of me. "I think you see that because you want to see it, Titan. I admire you for wanting to see the good in people when there isn't. That's a hard quality to come by. But I don't think Hunt deserves your doubt."

---

MY SCHEDULE WAS PACKED WITH MEETINGS, SO THE only time I was free to work on our presentation was in the evening. I wasn't going to invite him to my place, and his place was a war zone of reporters.

The office was the only neutral place.

All the lights were on when I stepped onto the floor, so I knew he was already there. My satchel was over my shoulder, and my Bullet was parked out front. When the traffic died down, it was fun to drive in the city. Feeling the powerful engine beneath my fingertips made me feel a little stronger.

I stepped into the conference room and found him sitting there, dressed down in jeans and a black t-shirt.

His hair was slightly messy because he'd obviously showered not too long ago. His chin was cleanly shaven, nothing but smooth skin around the hard jaw. His brown eyes were dark like the nighttime sky. Anytime he made a slight move, the fabric of his t-shirt hugged him perfectly. He was six-three of all muscle and man.

I needed to stop looking at him like that.

Hunt shifted his gaze to me, his dark eyes focusing on me like I was the only thing in the world. That intense expression was glued to mine. Now that he was no longer alone, all of his attention had been shifted to me. He didn't give a verbal greeting, his look saying a lot more than his mouth could.

God, I loved him.

I missed him.

I wished we were naked on this table, his powerful body thrusting into mine and making me his. I wanted to be his wife, to make love on top of the city we would own together. I wanted his come inside me every day, to be satisfied as no other man had ever satisfied me before.

Hunt watched me like he could read my thoughts.

I sat down and pretended it never happened. I acted like he didn't mean anything to me, like he was no one. Thorn's words came back to my mind, and I

couldn't ignore them. Hunt was a liar. He was dangerous. I didn't know the man I thought I loved.

I opened up my folders and set up my tablet.

He still didn't stop staring at me.

I refused to be affected by it. I refused to acknowledge it. "You want to start from the top?"

He worked his tight jaw, his mouth shifting
slightly under the tension. The angry look on his
face suggested he didn't want to be there. He was
frustrated with me, angry enough to fill the room.
But he was also anxious to run his fingers through
my hair, to brush his lips past mine in a long tease
before he actually kissed me. His desires filled the
room, the need for his hands to grab me, lift me onto
the table, and take me the way I wanted to be
taken. "Sure."

---

MY DRIVER ESCORTED ME FROM THE AIRPORT TO THE
resort on the coastline. I owned a home just a few
miles away, but since the conference was at the hotel, I
thought it would be easier to stay at the same place.
Making a strong appearance was important right now.
I wanted to be seen as often as possible, looking happy
and carefree in the beautiful Mediterranean. My

image as the weak victim of domestic abuse wouldn't last long.

I hoped Hunt could change his image as easily. People were far more involved in his story than they were in mine. Most of our associates here knew exactly who his father was. They'd probably even had lunch with him.

I checked in to my room and opened all the drapes. I had a prime view of the blue ocean and the sailboats in the harbor. The sun was bright, and the sea smelled like fresh salt. People were on the beach in their swimsuits, and a lot of women were topless. I had my own pool and a private patio, splurging for the nicest accommodations that were still available.

My phone lit up with a text message. *Heard you just arrived.*

I stared at Hunt's name and felt my throat tighten. I missed the way he kissed my neck. He used to smother me with kisses, drag his lips right over my pulse like an animal about to take a bite out of me. *How so?*

*You like to make an entrance. And people like to talk about it.*

I took my private plane in the middle of the night, sleeping through the journey in my luxurious king-size bed. I passed the night in a deep sleep and woke up to the sunshine in France. I was well-rested and ready to go.

*I'm at the bar with Bryan Thomas of NICO and Oliver Weston of Optimal Labs. Come down, and I'll introduce you.*

*I don't need you to introduce me.* If I wanted to meet someone, I'd walk up to them and shake their hand.

He was probably smiling at my comment. *Then let me introduce them to you.*

---

MIRANDA PETERSON AND I STOOD TOGETHER AT ONE OF the tables. She ran one of the biggest companies in the world, and her software program was installed on nearly all of my computers. She was older than I was, but down-to-earth and funny. Divorced with no kids, she was living the single life, but she seemed to be enjoying it. With black hair pulled into an elegant updo and a skintight dress, she was turning heads even in her late thirties. We'd run into each other at other events in Manhattan, and we always got along. I wouldn't call her a friend, but she was an associate I looked forward to seeing.

"I'm excited to hear your presentation." She sipped her martini with perfect posture, her shoulders back and her spine absolutely straight. She was classy and pretty, breaking the stereotype that beautiful women couldn't be smart too. "Diesel Hunt is a genius. With the two of you combined together, I can only imagine what you have in store."

"Yes, he is a brilliant man." When our personal relationship was put to the side, I had nothing but respect for him. He did business honorably, and he possessed the kind of intelligence that made even me feel intimidated.

"I've spoken to him a few times but never got to know him. What's he like?"

"Quiet. He doesn't say much."

She glanced at him on the other side of the room as he mingled with other entrepreneurs. "The strong and silent type. I picked up on that. Do you know if he's seeing someone? Since you see him every day, you must know."

I almost spat out my drink at the question. "Uh...I don't know. I don't think so."

"I'll make a pass later. I've been waiting for the right opportunity, but he's always talking to someone."

A flash of jealousy ripped through me that made me nearly shatter my glass. Her confidence annoyed me, but just a second ago I'd appreciated it. She and Hunt were nearly the same age, so the match was appropriate. She was smart and wealthy, just like I was. Not to mention, she was beautiful. They could spend the next few days enjoying the view from her room while they fucked in front of the window.

I took a big gulp of my drink, needing the alcohol more than ever.

"How are you and Thorn?"

I eyed Hunt, grateful that he was in deep conversation with two other men. His hands rested in the pockets of his slacks, and he wore a polite expression. It was nothing like the look he gave me, the one that was constantly full of intensity. His body looked thick and powerful in his clothes, and I knew he was turning more heads than Miranda's.

"Titan?"

"Sorry?" I turned back to her, my mouth on my glass again.

"How are you and Thorn?"

"Oh...we're great. He couldn't come because he had too much work at the office."

"That's too bad. Such a romantic place." She glanced at Hunt again.

I gripped my glass a little harder. Miranda was perfectly within her rights to be interested in Hunt—a single man. But I couldn't help but feel the jealousy, which was ridiculous because it was unrealistic to expect any straight woman not to gawk over him.

"He's moving to the bar." Miranda stepped away from me, prepared to intercept Hunt. "Wish me luck."

No.

She approached Hunt when he reached the counter, and she opened with a line that made him laugh.

I took another drink, almost running on empty. My feet started to hurt in my heels, and I was hit with an unexpected wave of heat. How would I get through this trip if they were hooking up every night? How would I be able to swallow the devastation of knowing some other woman was enjoying him?

When I'd enjoyed him for so long.

Hunt pivoted his body against the counter and focused on Miranda while her back was turned to me.

I shouldn't stare, but I couldn't help it.

Hunt's eyes shifted slightly to me just an inch from her face. His gaze remained glued there during the conversation; it was painfully obvious he was staring at me and not her. She probably couldn't tell the difference because we were in the same line of sight.

My pulse quickened. My mouth went dry.

He didn't blink. He said very little to her, giving a slight nod here and there.

All of his focus was on me.

Finally, the conversation ended. Hunt got his drink, and Miranda walked back toward me. She still wore a smile and an elegant posture, so it seemed like she got the answer she wanted.

Maybe she did.

"How'd it go?" My eyes glanced at Hunt's back.

She set down her drink with a sigh. "Said he's seeing someone."

My eyes darted to her face. "He did?"

"Yeah. Said it's pretty serious. Why am I not surprised? A man like that doesn't stay on the market long."

"Yeah..." When my eyes turned back to him, I was greeted with that intense gaze. He stood there alone where anyone could watch him, but he didn't seem to care about getting caught looking straight at me. He drank his Old Fashioned as he looked at me, those dark eyes complementing the liquid sitting in his glass. He kept drinking and drinking as he kept watching and watching.

I was the first one to break eye contact because I couldn't handle it anymore.

He won.

AFTER MIDNIGHT, SOMEONE KNOCKED ON THE DOOR.

I knew who it was. I'd have to be completely clueless not to figure it out. And I also knew exactly what would happen if I opened the door. Touches would turn to kisses. Words would turn to moans. Clothes would drop, and he would be plunged deep inside me for the rest of the night.

It was smart to ignore it, to pretend I was asleep and hadn't heard it. Watching him blow off another beautiful woman for me made my thighs squeeze together tightly. It tricked my heart into believing him, believing that he really loved me from head to toe.

I wished he loved me.

I could stand in a room with all my peers with the most amazing man on my arm. I wouldn't have to lie about my feelings. Every time I looked at him, I knew he would already be looking at me with that possessive gaze. I could be in love for all the world to see.

But he betrayed me. I had to keep reminding myself of that.

But the doubt, lust, and love crept in.

He knocked again.

Don't open that door, Titan.

Just ignore it.

Hunt didn't knock again, but his message popped up on my phone. *Baby.*

I took a deep breath and closed my eyes at the same time, like I'd actually heard him say the word. Like the sound left his lips and landed on my ear because we were right next to each other.

I sat on the edge of the bed and squeezed my thighs together as I pictured the kiss he would give me if I opened the door.

*I'm not going anywhere.*

Fuck.

He tapped his knuckles against the door for a third time.

My legs automatically brought me to my feet, and I walked to the door, still wearing my stilettos even though I'd been in my room for nearly an hour. I'd finished up drinks with a few associates then slipped away before Hunt could realize I was gone.

I moved to the door and pressed my forehead against it, knowing he was just on the other side. If I held my breath, I could hear his presence on the other side of the door. I could hear him shift slightly, hear his breath of frustration. Even if I hadn't been able to hear him, I could feel him. Like a magnetic field was just on the other side, I could feel the pull through a solid object—because Hunt was the most powerful solid object in the building.

My hand moved to the doorknob.

"Open it," he whispered into the crack. "Or I will."

I finally turned the knob and cracked the door open, just enough to see his face. I planned to tell him to leave, that I was tired and needed to rest. But when I saw those brooding brown eyes, I couldn't think of anything coherent to say.

He pushed the door open and stepped inside, immediately crowding me backward.

I should stand my ground and order him to leave. I had the power if I wanted it. Even when I felt like he was in control, I could always take it back. All I had to do was straighten my spine and harden my resolve.

But that didn't happen.

He crowded me farther into the room, forcing me to move back as he took up all the space. He was in the same suit he wore in the bar, black with a black tie. He looked like a million bucks. All he was missing was a big red bow, and he would be the best Christmas present. "Hunt—"

"You may not be mine. But I'm still yours."

Just like that, the air was taken from my lungs. All the power I'd attained through years of ruthlessness disappeared. It evaporated into thin air like it never existed in the first place. He stripped away my power.

His hand moved to my cheek and slowly slid into my hair. His callused fingertips brushed across my skin as they secured a place in my strands. He pressed his face close to mine and tilted my gaze to meet his. His warm breath fell on my skin, his breath heavy with whiskey. I recognized it because it was practically water to me. I'd recognize it anywhere.

He pressed his forehead to mine and closed his eyes, his other hand getting a firm grip on my hip. It slowly slid to my waist where he clutched me harder through the silk fabric of my dress. "I don't want her. I don't want that woman in the club. You know what I want?"

I closed my eyes and felt his fingers dig into my neck.

"I want to make love to you. I want to fuck you. I want to bury all my desire, all my anger, deep between your legs. I want to sink you into the mattress as I conquer you, as I bury my entire cock inside that pussy. I want to tell you I love you while you scream it back to me. I want you to forget these lies you've heard about me and just give in to me. I want you to spread your legs, grab my ass, and pull me harder into you even though you can't take anymore. I want it just to be us...nothing else." His fingers wrapped around my hair, and he got a tighter grip on me, holding me like a horse with reins.

I breathed against his mouth, feeling his arousal

burning into my skin. Now that the words were in the air and I was soaked between my legs, I couldn't see straight. All I wanted was exactly what he promised. "Fuck me."

His hand dug under the fall of my hair, and he sealed his mouth over mine. He cocked his head, tilting his face so our lips could take one another perfectly. He tugged on my hair as he inched me backward, directing me to the large bed I wouldn't have to enjoy alone. His fingers moved to the back of my dress, and he tugged the zipper to the top of my ass. It fell off my shoulders and landed around my heels. My tits were covered with tape to hide my nipples, and he tugged each one off my skin, making both of my nipples ache as the sticky material was removed. He broke our kiss to pull my thong down my long legs. He sprinkled a few kisses along my thighs on the way down. When he rose to his full height, he yanked off his tie and dropped it on top of my panties. His eyes roamed over my naked body, staring at the perkiness of my breasts, the hollow in my throat, and my slender waistline as his fingers worked the buttons of his shirt. He popped each one open, staring at me like a hungry man who just ordered everything on the menu. When his shirt was finally open, he let it slide off his shoulders and onto the floor.

His chiseled physique was as sexy as I remembered. Massive pectoral muscles covered his chest. He was broad on top and slim around the hips. He was the perfect inverted triangle, the ultimate symbol of masculinity. He was man enough to make me feel like pure woman, even when I didn't always exhibit the most feminine traits. His tanned skin was hairless, and there were shadows across his stomach from the crevices of his abs. He was perfect, all muscle, skin, and tendons.

My lips automatically parted so I could get more air, and my tongue swiped across my bottom lip. The last thing I was thinking about was the scandal he'd released to the media, of the photograph of him and that woman. All I was thinking about was unfiltered, unbridled lust.

He loosened his belt and got his pants undone. They slid down his muscular thighs until they were on the floor with the rest of our clothing. He kicked off his shoes and pulled off his socks. When he was completely nude, he looked like a statue of a Roman soldier. He was powerful, timeless, beautiful. As hard as his body was, his chiseled jaw and dark eyes were harder. Nothing could compare to that forceful expression, that look that brought countless women to their knees.

I wanted to be on my knees now.

I lowered myself to the floor, my knees hitting our mutual pile of clothing. My hands gripped his muscular thighs for balance, and I pressed my lips to the base of his cock, the shaft of steel that was already drooling for me at the tip. I gave him a soft kiss then a swipe of my tongue.

Hunt's piercing expression didn't change as his hand glided into my hair and gripped the back of my neck.

I felt the thick vein along his length as I moved up, slowly inching to the tip where he was oozing for me. I moved farther until I reached the head.

Hunt held his breath as he waited for me to taste him.

I swiped my tongue over the lubricated flesh and brought the taste into my mouth. He tasted exactly the way I remembered. I brought his tip into my mouth and sucked, getting as much of him as I could.

His lidded eyes fell as he moaned.

I pushed him to the back of my throat, feeling him stretch my throat and cheeks. Saliva immediately began to shift in my mouth as it soaked into his skin and moved to my lips. I flattened my tongue to cushion him and slowly moved back and forth, his cock fucking my mouth.

He gripped my neck tighter and positioned himself closer to me, giving me more of his length even though it would never fit completely inside me. "Missed my cock, baby?"

My mouth was full so I couldn't speak. I looked him in the eye with my mouth gaping open. I gave a slight nod.

His fingers dug into me harder, and his hips started to thrust. He fucked my mouth with his cock and fucked the rest of me with his eyes. His breathing picked up, heavy and sexy.

I could suck his dick all day, but I wanted to feel him between my legs, to feel him stretching me like he used to.

He pulled his dripping cock out of my mouth and raised me to my feet by the neck. Instead of throwing me on the bed, he gripped my ass with his big hands, and he lifted me to his waist. With one arm circled around me, he grabbed his cock and pointed it at my entrance. He slowly lowered me onto his length, his massive tip stretching my entrance and the rest of my channel. He sank deeper into me, pushing until he was plunged deep inside me. He held me against him with ease, my arms hooked around his neck as our faces pressed together.

I dug my nails into his shoulders and moaned

right in his face, missing how good this felt. His muscular arms held my entire weight effortlessly, his biceps clenching and his triceps tight. He stood tall in the center of the room, holding me at a height I wasn't used to experiencing, even in heels.

His cock pulsed inside me, savoring the feel of my wet tightness. He brushed his nose against mine, a masculine moan erupting from deep inside his throat. "Fuck." His arms were hooked underneath my spread thighs, and he gripped my ass cheeks. His breathing didn't escalate, and he didn't show a sign of exertion. He held me like I weighed nothing at all.

There was nothing sexier than seeing him stand there, his reflection in the mirror on the opposite wall. His ass was tight, the muscles of his back rippling, and his firm thighs were thick. He was the perfect example of power and strength. I'd never seen a more purely masculine sight in my life. I'd never been so full of a man. I'd never been swept off my feet—literally.

He started to move me up and down, dragging my pussy from the base of his cock all the way to the head. I was so slick that I could hear the sounds our bodies made as they moved together. He was thick and I was tight. It made for perfect fucking.

He watched my expression as he moved inside me, his eyes locked on mine. Sometimes, he looked at my lips. Sometimes, he brushed his nose against mine. He fucked me and made love to me at the same time, letting me dig my nails as deep as I wanted. He didn't kiss me, probably wanting to watch my reaction to him instead.

He felt so good. He'd never felt this good. I used his shoulders to lift myself up and down even though he didn't need the help. He carried me like a weightless doll. He sheathed his cock inside me like I was a sex toy, not a heavy human being.

I could feel myself grow wetter and tighter, my tiny pussy riding his length so intensely. Every thrust felt better than the previous. I could stay like this forever, lifted and carried like I weighed nothing to him. The angle was deep, and he plunged himself far inside me every single time. He had complete access to me, and he took advantage of it with every thrust.

I didn't want to come so quickly. It would be a dead giveaway that I missed him, that I missed it when he fucked me like this. I hadn't been with anyone else. I hadn't even been with my hand. Over a week had passed, and I hadn't gotten any action whatsoever. My body practically cried with joy.

He brushed his lips over mine. "Come, baby."

Instead of being ashamed that Hunt knew me so well, I felt another rush of arousal. He knew everything about my body, knew exactly how to please a woman, and he could feel the desires between my legs. I clung to him harder as the heat spread over me like a wildfire. I burned everywhere, white-hot and scorching. My deep pants turned into screams. "Diesel..." My fingers dug deep into his hair.

He yanked me onto his length at an increased speed, hitting me deep and hard over and over. He plunged inside me, giving me all of him. His actions made my orgasm stretch on forever, making it last.

I couldn't remember the last time I came this hard. It was the kind of orgasm that made me want to cry. Tears sprung to my eyes, and my lips quivered in ecstasy. It felt so good, so satisfying. Hunt watched my expression all the way through, the corner of his mouth raised in a slightly arrogant smile. His eyes carried the same sharp intensity, the same heated desire that nearly burned my face.

The orgasm slowly flowed away, drifting from my body and making me feel tender everywhere. My body released another wave of moisture, and now Hunt was so wet he was soaked. I pressed my forehead to his and felt the unbreakable connection between us, the bond I couldn't shake. He was supposed to mean nothing to me, but ever since the day I met him, he'd changed my world.

He buried himself to the hilt then carried me to the bed. Effortlessly, he held me with one arm as he lowered my head to the pillow and remained deep inside me. His cock was pulsing, throbbing. He pinned my legs back with his arms and held himself over me, his cock plunging inside me.

Now I wanted to come again.

He kissed me softly on the mouth, his lips moving against mine with scorching passion. He didn't move within me, his thick cock resting deep inside my pussy. Just when he gave me some tongue, he pulled away. "This is how I want to come inside you." He shifted his weight forward, making me dip into the mattress. The pillow pushed around my head, and the sheets hugged my body. I was pinned down and dominated, my body open for Hunt to take. I was a prisoner and he was my captor, but I didn't want to run away. "Grab my ass."

My hands snaked to his muscular cheeks.

He started to thrust inside me, pushing his fat cock as deep as my body would allow.

I yanked on his ass at the same time, pulling him farther inside me. With every thrust, I felt him grind against my clit. My pussy was ready for his seed, and the anticipation of his orgasm made me come again.

"Diesel..." My nails dug into his skin, and I widened my legs farther.

"Wider."

I opened my legs as far as they would go.

He moaned as he continued his thrusts, my pussy completely available to him. He didn't increase his pace, keeping his strokes slow and even. His eyes darkened noticeably, staying focused on mine. His cock started to thicken inside me, pulsing with anticipation.

He held his breath as he stopped moving, his length completely inside me. He moaned with his release, dumping all of his desire deep between my legs. He closed his eyes for a moment as he enjoyed it, a flush of desire overcoming him.

I continued to grip his ass, feeling the weight from all of his come. It was heavy and warm. It felt incredible, an experience I used to take for granted. I felt his seed drip from my entrance and seep between my cheeks to the sheets. He gave me so much that it wouldn't fit entirely within me.

"Fuck..." My ankles locked together at his lower back, and I hooked my arms around his neck. I pressed my forehead to his, feeling his softening cock inside me. More come dripped out, but I wasn't in a hurry to move.

I wanted to stay just like this. All the chaos in my

heart died away. The world didn't seem so crazy anymore. Hunt had hurt me, and I still didn't know who I was really dealing with. But when we were together, I didn't think about the doubt or the pain. All I thought about was this man.

This man buried deep in my heart.

WE SPENT the next few hours in bed, going at it without saying more than a few words to each other. My heart finally stopped cracking now that I was buried deep inside her. I didn't only want her because she was the most beautiful woman in every room I walked into. I wanted to be inside her because it felt so good…feeling her heart beat in tune with mine. We were connected again, our undeniable attraction pulling us into a single person.

If Miranda had made a move on me in the past, I would have said yes in a heartbeat. She was beautiful, classy, and successful. I wouldn't mind spending a week in the sack with her. But since Titan had walked into my life, my attraction to other women was nonexistent. I didn't think about sex unless Titan was associated with it. Women were just pretty men, nothing more. Why would I want to be with Miranda when I was in love with Titan?

I was actually pissed when she hit on me.

I was pissed that I couldn't just tell her I was seeing Titan.

I had to lie and say I was seeing someone else while my eyes were glued to the woman to whom I was referring. My arm should have been around her waist. My fingers should have been wrapped around her wrist. I should have been the one getting her something to drink from the bar. All the men in that room should have been jealous of me, not Thorn.

Pissed me the fuck off.

When we were finished and her pussy was stuffed with more come than she could handle, I grabbed my clothes from the floor and got dressed. As much as I wanted to sleep beside her, I knew Titan wouldn't go for it. She'd probably regret sleeping with me the second the haze disappeared from her eyes. She would regret this night because she was supposed to stay away from me.

I had to give her a false sense of security.

Her heart was still weak for me, and she still wanted me despite the lies she'd heard. When I told her it wasn't me, she wanted to believe me. I could see the look in her eyes as she listened to me. Her fortifications were weak. She softened anytime she heard my voice. But with all the damning evidence against me, she didn't welcome me with open arms. She was on edge, wanting to believe me but refusing to do so.

I understood. Anyone else would have done the same thing.

There was still hope for us.

But I couldn't push it. If I pressed her for more, she would just turn me down again. She would reevaluate the situation but come to the same decision. Her brilliant mind would tell her I couldn't be trusted. She already gave me all of herself, and after the way she was hurt and humiliated, she couldn't do it again.

I couldn't rush this. I had to revert back to what we used to be, two people only interested in sex. Everything else would fall back into place if I was patient enough. The truth would come out. It always did.

I left my tie undone around my neck and turned to her on the bed.

She sat up with the sheets pulled over her chest even though I'd spent the last few hours staring at her tits. She didn't ask me to stay, and that told me all of my theories were correct.

"Good night." I turned to the door.

Her quiet voice followed behind me. "Good night."

I walked out and stepped into my room right next

door. She didn't know we were neighbors yet. I'd asked for our rooms to be side by side since we were business partners. The hotel accommodated the request immediately.

Now that I was back in my room alone, I didn't feel tired. I hopped into the shower and rinsed off before I came back into the luxurious room that was identical to Titan's. I made myself a drink and sat on the couch in my boxers.

I'd felt a brief moment of happiness with Titan, but now it'd been taken away from me. A thick wall was back between us. I left like we'd had a one-night stand that would never be discussed again. I stirred my drink and took another sip, feeling the misery sink into my bones. I wanted to be in that bed with her, listening to her breathing change as she fell asleep.

But I was sitting alone in the dark—only my drink for company.

---

MARSHALL TUCKER AND I WERE FRIENDS. WE'D PARTIED together a few times, picked up a few women in Los Angeles and spent the evening in his mansion in Hollywood. He was a playboy like I was...or used to be.

We had lunch at the restaurant at the resort, sitting

on the patio and looking at the sailboats sprinkled across the blue water. Other associates attending the conference were there, including Miranda Peterson. She was sitting at a different table with some of her assistants.

Marshall was in a pale blue collared shirt with dark jeans. Sunglasses sat on the bridge of his nose, and his skin was tanned, probably from spending a lot of time in the California sun. The top button of his shirt was open, revealing a muscular chest. He just hit forty a few months ago, but that hadn't worn down his youth. "Now that you've told me business is doing well and your life is pretty spectacular...I feel like I have to ask about that interview." He gave me a slight shrug in apology. "It was bound to come up, right?"

So far, no one had asked me about it, probably because they knew I wouldn't answer. Or they just didn't want to piss me off. "Not much to say. The interview covered it all."

Marshall gave a slight nod. "Gotcha. Sorry I brought it up."

"It's alright."

"I heard you acquired Megaland. That's a strong company."

"It is. I've already made a lot of progress with it. The guys running the company with me are very bright. They've got a lot of ideas and a lot of product for me to sell. I think we're going to take up most of the space in the tech industry."

"Good for you. Looks like the only area you haven't covered is sports." He chuckled before he took a drink of his beer.

It'd crossed my mind. I just hadn't had time. "Not enough hours in the day."

"Definitely." He clinked his glass against mine. "I'll drink to that." He brought his glass to his lips as his eyes glanced to the entryway of the restaurant. He took a long drink as he focused his eyes on the subject, staying put. He put his glass down without watching what he was doing.

A man only possessed that stare when he was looking at a woman.

I didn't turn around to check who'd stolen his fascination.

Marshall turned his gaze back on me. "Your business partner just walked in."

My eyes narrowed when I connected the dots. I'd seen him fuck women with my own eyes. I knew exactly what that look meant—and I didn't appreciate it.

"Should we invite her over?" he asked. "She seems to be alone." When his eyes turned back to her, his look shifted downward, probably staring at her legs.

I wanted to choke him to death. "Look at her like that again, and see what happens."

Marshall looked at me again, but he wore a smile like he thought I was joking.

"Not kidding." I rose from the seat and turned to the hostess stand. Titan was standing there in a baby-blue sundress and brown sandals. Her long hair was in big curls, and she'd done her makeup just the way I liked. She looked like she belonged on my yacht, sailing the Mediterranean with me while we fucked and drank under the sun.

Her eyes turned to me, and like always, they softened slightly. The movement was hardly noticeable, and unless someone knew what it meant, they wouldn't understand it. It was a look she only gave to me—because she was still head over heels for me.

Like I was for her.

I walked up to her and circled my arm around her waist. I leaned in and kissed her on the cheek.

She stilled at the affection, knowing it wasn't a meaningless greeting between associates. It was a possessive touch, one that I was doing just for Marshall to see. He thought she was seeing Thorn, but that didn't change anything.

She was my girl.

And I didn't let anyone look at my girl like that.

She pulled away, slight color coming into her cheeks. She tried to brush off the tingling sensation I knew she was feeling deep inside her chest, but she couldn't. I read her expression as easily as an open book.

"Would you like to join us?" I stepped back and nodded to the table.

"Sure." She righted herself the second I stopped touching her, changing back into Tatum Titan. She hardened her gaze, straightened her spine, and turned into the tallest person on the patio. "Who's your friend?"

"Marshall Tucker." He had a handsome face with a ripped physique. Not to mention, he had money. But I wasn't threatened by him. If she had slept with him, Marshall probably wouldn't have checked her out so vigorously. And it's not like he had a chance with her now—not while I was living and breathing.

"Never met him."

We returned to the table, and I made the introductions. "Titan, this is my friend, Marshall Tucker."

He smiled as he grabbed her hand, gripping her wrist and holding it for a little too long. "It's nice to meet you. I feel like I already know you."

"You too. I'm familiar with your work. I have a policy with your life insurance group."

He winked. "Smart girl."

We sat down, and I ordered Titan an Old Fashioned.

Titan flashed me a glare, probably annoyed that I ordered for her when she was perfectly capable of doing it herself. But she didn't voice her annoyance when Marshall was so close.

"I didn't know you guys knew each other so well," Marshall said. "I've never heard you talk about her."

"We didn't become associates until recently." That was the only explanation I would give him.

"You seem close." Marshall's comment was purely friendly, but he didn't understand the kind of impact it had on both of us. "I've never seen Hunt pull out a chair for anyone or order a drink for someone, not even when we were partying with those two models in Laguna Hills."

If Titan was jealous, she hid it. She didn't have any reaction at all, putting on a brave face and pretending his words meant nothing to her. She was an expert at deceiving people—except me. I couldn't be fooled. "I've taught him some manners since we started working together."

Marshall chuckled.

"No," I said. "I just actually like you, Titan."

She didn't hide her reaction as well that time, covering up her expression by taking a drink.

"You don't like me?" Marshall teased. "You never pull out the chair for me."

"Turn into a lady, and I might," I countered.

Marshall chuckled again. "You straightened him out, Titan. He's like a completely different man since the last time I saw him."

My eyes shifted to her face. "That's because I am."

She held my gaze a brief second longer than she should, and that was a dead giveaway that she understood my intention perfectly. She turned away and looked at Marshall as she drank from her glass.

Marshall pivoted his body slightly toward her, far more interested in her than he was in me. I'd given him a firm warning that he shouldn't mess with Titan, and I hoped he took me seriously. Friends or not, I'd beat the shit out of him for giving her anything but his respect. "How do you like working with someone else? You usually fly solo, right?"

Titan knew the question was reserved for her. "Hunt brings a lot to the table. I couldn't ask for a better partner with more experience. He's more familiar with the industry, so it's great to have him on board."

"Really?" he asked. "I'm surprised you need him at all."

"I think there's always more to learn," she said coolly.

"You flatter me," I said.

"And you?" Marshall asked me. "How do you like it?"

"She's Tatum Titan," I said simply. "Couldn't ask for anyone better."

The corner of her mouth rose in a smile. "You flatter me."

I instinctively wanted to reach out my hand and rest it on top of hers, but I wasn't allowed to do such a thing in public. I was forced to restrain myself, to keep up the pretense that I only cared about what was in her brain, not between her legs.

In reality, I cared about both.

"Thorn isn't jealous, is he?" Marshall asked.

"Why should he be?" Titan asked. "He works with businesswomen all the time, and I never bat an eye over it."

"Well, none of them are you," he said with a grin. "And Hunt is a pretty good-looking guy."

I was getting tired of these sexually motivated statements. "Marshall."

His eyes flicked to me.

"What did we just talk about?"

His smile slowly fell when he realized I was dead serious.

Titan's eyes shifted back and forth between us as she held her glass in her hand.

I held his stare and refused to blink, overriding him as much as possible.

He was the first to turn away and cover up his scowl with his drink.

Titan picked up on the tension, but she dissipated it effortlessly. "I saw that your company is doing really well in the market right now. Your dividends are pretty impressive."

Once Marshall was flattered by a genius like Tatum Titan, he switched gears. "Thanks. My team does a lot of research into real estate..." Once he was on the topic of business, he stuck to it—like glue.

---

WE ENTERED THE CONFERENCE AND MINGLED WITH A few associates. I stuck to Titan's side because I wanted to be there—not because I felt obligated. People were obviously talking about our respective stories that had been splashed across the media, but the longer they saw us together as a united front, the more it would give them something appropriate to talk about.

Now Titan was in her pencil skirt and tight blouse, wearing sky-high heels like they were slippers. She grabbed a pamphlet off a table and browsed through it.

I stood beside her, looking at the schedule over her shoulder. We weren't giving our presentation until tomorrow, so we got to enjoy the work everyone else was doing. These conferences provided great opportunities for networking. I wasn't looking for more relationships, but if I did a favor for someone, they usually did me a favor somewhere down the road.

And sometimes it paid off.

She didn't turn her eyes to me, staring at the schedule. "I don't need you to stick up for me like that, Hunt."

My gaze shifted to her profile, seeing her long eyelashes peek out and curl toward the ceiling. They were thick and black, her makeup usually heavy around the eyes. It gave her a distinct look of feminine perfection as well as sexy authority. She hypnotized with her lustrous look. I wondered if she was aware of the effect she had on people. "I know."

"Then don't do it." She turned the page over and looked at the other side.

"It's a bad habit."

"When did it become a habit?" she asked quietly.

My hand moved to her waist, the touch still somewhat professional. "You know when it became a habit." My lips were close to her ear, almost close enough to brush across her skin. "I know Marshall. That guy only has one thing on his mind. I see the way he looks at you, and I don't like it."

"Get used to it," she said. "There's nothing you can do about it. Men will look. It's not a crime."

"It is a crime when you belong to me."

She turned her face up and looked at me, that flash of provoked irritation bright in her eyes. But underneath that expression was that fire I saw last night, that burning desire for as much of my cock as she could take. "Hunt."

"We both know what's going to happen later tonight. So let's stop pretending." My hand squeezed her waist gently before I dropped it and stepped away. She probably still held the furious look in her eyes, but there was nothing she could do about it.

She knew I was right.

I took a seat in one of the back rows and waited for the presentation to begin. A group of guys in the fitness space had an app that would revolutionize the industry. I'd heard about them, and I was curious to learn everything I could about the topic. I never attended the seminars I was already well-acquainted with. I only went to the ones I knew nothing about—so I could learn something.

Marshall dropped into the seat beside me. "What the hell was that about?"

I rested my ankle on the opposite knee and glanced at my watch, seeing we had a few minutes before we began.

"Hunt, you can hear me."

"I know. I'm just ignoring you."

"What's your deal? Why are you a dick when Titan comes into the picture?"

"I don't like you talking about her like that. I told you that already."

"I didn't say anything about her."

"Don't play stupid with me." I turned my expression on him, cold and dark. "You eye-fucked the shit out of her."

"Well, look at her."

My hand tightened into a fist.

Marshall caught the movement and raised both eyebrows. "Hunt, what's the deal? I've never heard you defend someone's honor before. I distinctly remember two women fighting to give you head in the hotel room in Beverly Hills."

That was a long time ago. "She's important to me. She's obviously not interested in you, so treat her with some respect."

"What makes you think she's not interested?"

I'd never punched someone during a conference. Maybe today would be my first time. "Because she's not, Marshall. She's with Thorn." I hated saying that out loud, the lie that the world had been tricked to believe.

"I never see them together, so who knows how serious they are."

"They're both devoted to their work. Nothing wrong with that." I turned back to the front.

He rested his arm over the back of the chair. "You know what I think?"

I ignored the sneer on his face.

"I think you have a thing for her."

I didn't deny it because I didn't want to do that anymore. Titan wanted me to lie to the world, but I was tired of it. She pretended I meant nothing to her, and I pretended she was just a business associate that didn't turn my head every time she walked in a room. Not only was I attracted to her, but I admired her for the incredible woman that she was. I was tired of hiding my awe, my obvious affection for her. "Maybe I do."

Marshall's eyes narrowed, and a grin stretched across his face. "You have expensive taste."

"Classy taste."

"If I'd known you called dibs on her, I wouldn't have been such an ass."

"You shouldn't be an ass anyway."

"Duly noted," he said with a smile. "What are you going to do about Thorn?"

"Nothing."

"Are you going to tell her?"

"No. I'm sure she knows."

"Yeah," he said. "You do make it obvious. So what are you going to do?"

"I don't know. Nothing I can do."

"You think she's in love with Thorn?" he asked. "Sometimes I think it's just a glorified business arrangement. When I see them touch in public, it doesn't seem genuine." Marshall wasn't a billionaire by being an idiot.

"I don't know what to think. But I respect her relationship."

"If you say so."

The presentation started, so we fell silent and looked to the front of the room.

---

TITAN WAS CHITCHATTING WITH ONE OF THE MEMBERS of the board of directors of the biggest retailer in the world, Climax. They sold edgy clothes, shoes, and accessories. Titan had invaded the beauty cosmetics industry. In fact, she owned all of it. It's where most of her wealth came from. She didn't just make good decisions regarding her product, she was a brilliant marketer. She made women realize they needed her products just as much as they needed food and water.

A damn genius.

She held her glass of champagne as she smiled and listened to his words. The bubbles were rising to the surface, and every few seconds, she took a drink. The gleam from the liquor shone in her eyes, and I wondered if I would taste it later tonight.

Marshall came up to me and nudged me in the side. "Guess what?"

"What?" My eyes stayed on Titan.

"I met a few models this afternoon. They're from Milan, but they're staying in France for a spa getaway. Trust me when I say they can destroy a runway."

If we were having a bragging contest, there was one woman I'd love to boast about. "Have fun."

"Don't be stupid," he said. "You're coming along. They're in my suite upstairs. They're already liquored up and ready to go."

Titan finished her conversation with the man before her eyes found me. She walked across the room, her posture perfect and her fingertips gripping the stem of the glass. She couldn't have picked a worse time to join us.

"I'm gonna pass, Marshall. But thanks for the invite."

"Did you hear what I said?" he asked incredulously. "They're models."

"I've been with lots of models. So what?" I turned back to Titan, who now wore a guarded expression. She'd walked in at the wrong time, and judging from her discomfort, she knew about it.

"Yes. I remember those two women taking turns sucking you off," he said. "But wouldn't you want to repeat that?" He didn't seem to notice Titan was standing there because he was too absorbed in this conversation about getting laid. Now his eyes shifted her way, but he didn't appear embarrassed that she'd heard it.

Titan knew what kind of man I was before she came along. That didn't mean I wanted her to know the specifics of my glamorous sex life. It was redundant and boring. The sparks didn't really ignite until she walked into my life.

Until Tatum Titan entered my bed.

Titan took a long drink of her champagne, trying to cover up the burn in her cheeks.

"Marshall," I said firmly. "You can handle them on your own." I patted him on the shoulder.

"I don't like this version of Hunt." He patted my arm back a little harder, clearly annoyed with my decision. "I'll be in my suite if you change your mind." He nodded to Titan before he walked away.

Now it was just her and me.

Thinking about that joint blow job I received last year.

I looked into her eyes and saw her look into mine. She couldn't hide her jealousy as much as she tried. I could see it—deep down inside. When she heard about me kissing that woman in the club, she'd worn the exact same expression. She took another drink to compose herself, doing her best to appear indifferent to the news she just heard. "You're free to do what you want, Hunt."

"And I'm doing exactly what I want."

"No, you aren't. You hooked up with that woman last week, and now you have a team of women wanting to take turns giving you a blow job. Don't let me stop you." She kept her voice steady as if she weren't mad, but there was no mistaking the hurt in her expression.

She was jealous. Furiously jealous. I liked it enough to smile, but I stopped my lip from curling. "You aren't stopping me. You know I wasn't with that woman."

"I know you said you weren't with her...but that doesn't mean anything."

"I'm not a liar, Titan."

She looked away. "Maybe you are. Maybe you aren't."

"You don't want me to go upstairs. I don't want to go upstairs either. So let's just go back to your room and do what we really want." My hands were in my pockets, but I leaned in close to her, our proximity inappropriate for two platonic friends.

She finished her glass and swallowed hard, stalling her answer. "The only thing I want to do is get away from you."

"Really?" I challenged. "So you couldn't care less if I joined Marshall."

She looked me right in the eye, her gaze steady. "Not in the least." She did her best to appear sincere, but it wasn't enough.

I didn't believe her. "Then I'll go."

She pressed her lips tightly together. "Fine."

"Fine." I met her hard look with my own before I turned my back on her. I walked out of the lobby and directly into the elevator. When I turned around and looked at her, she had her back turned to me, her arms crossed over her chest.

I stared at her until the doors closed.

---

I SAT ON THE COUCH AND HELPED MYSELF TO THE whiskey and ice cubes. I poured a drink and enjoyed it as I looked at the view outside. There wasn't much to see because the sun was gone, but the lights along the walkway were beautiful. The sailboats in the harbor weren't visible, but as soon as morning arrived, they would be bobbing on the ocean.

The keycard machine in the door lit up, and the knob turned as Titan stepped inside. I'd known she would retreat to her room within ten minutes after our conversation was over. She kicked off her heels, tossed her clutch aside, and judging from the way she jerked, she was angry as she moved through the suite.

She didn't notice me.

She sighed and ran her fingers through her hair, and the sound she made with her lips was painful to listen to. All of her heartbreak was uttered in the single sound, her devastation at the thought of me being with two beautiful women instead of her.

Listening to her sadness made me feel terrible because I knew I really did hurt her. Well, I didn't. But she thought I did. "Care for a drink?"

She froze at the sound of my voice, her lithe body rigid with surprise. She slowly turned toward me, her makeup slightly smeared because of the damp emotion in her eyes. She couldn't fix it with me sitting right there, so she left it alone.

I set my drink on the table, the glass thudding against the surface. It was so quiet in the room I could hear every single sound. I could hear every single time she took a breath. The air moved past her lips, into her lungs, and back out again.

Despite being caught in the act, she held my gaze like she had nothing to be ashamed of.

I rose to my feet and met her head on, wanting to wipe away that look of pain.

She held my gaze until she couldn't look at me anymore, the emotion too raw. She was relieved I was there but embarrassed that it was plainly obvious how she felt—that she was hopelessly in love with me. She ran her fingers through her hair and looked at the floor, a foot shorter than she usually was without her stilettos.

I moved closer to her, and she breathed deeper when I drew near. My hand slid into her hair, and I forced her gaze up, making her look directly into my eyes. Now she couldn't hide from me. I could see everything she didn't want me to see; I could see her agony as well as her desire. "Don't ever tell me to leave if you want me to stay." I positioned her head perfectly so I could place my mouth against her soft lips. It was a gentle kiss, so soft our mouths hardly moved together. She breathed into my mouth, and I took everything she offered me, sucking her essence deep inside my chest. "Tell me."

Her fingers wrapped around my wrist, and she kissed me back, deepening the embrace. "Stay."

My arm tightened around her waist, and I pulled her hard against me, feeling her perky tits against my chest. I squeezed her harder than I should, but I needed all of her, everything I could get. I was ticked she would think, even for a second, I would go to some other woman's bed for the night. Ever since I met Titan, she'd become my obsession. I had everything I could possibly want in the world, but she was the only thing I truly valued. Money, cars, mansions...none of those gave me happiness.

Only she did.

My hand tightened into a fist as I squeezed the fabric of her dress, making my forearm flex around her waist. My other hand demolished her hair, gripping it like it was a lasso and she was my prey.

She breathed harder into my mouth, matching my intensity almost instantly. When she kissed me, she trembled slightly right against my mouth. Moans mixed with breaths as she fell deeper into me, giving herself over to me. She didn't try to hide her feelings anymore. She wanted me there with her, plowing between her legs for the entire night. She didn't want to share me with anyone else. She wanted to be the only woman I fucked—the only woman I loved.

Her dress dropped to the floor, and her bra was snapped off. I tugged her panties down her ass, feeling the steep swell of the impressive piece of muscle. She got my jacket and collared shirt off so she could run her hands over my expansive chest. She fell into her typically voracious attitude, yanking off my belt and undoing my slacks. She pushed everything down, getting me naked as quickly as possible.

Before I could scoop her up and carry her to the bed, she pushed me back onto the mattress. I had been the one controlling the situation, but she didn't hesitate to take over once she hit her stride.

I lay back and scooted toward the headboard, knowing she wanted to ride my fat dick. It was one of her favorite things to do—and it was one of my favorite things to watch.

She crawled onto my lap and straddled my hips, her beautiful tits against my chest. With hard nipples and a beautiful blush across her skin, she had the perfect rack. Her tits were big, but they were perfectly shaped. They were gorgeous and delicious.

Her folds sat right on my cock, her wet pussy soaking my length. Her beautiful brown hair cascaded over her shoulders, uneven and disheveled from my aggressive hand. With slightly parted lips and sex in her eyes, she looked like my fantasy. She was the exact kind of woman I wanted to fuck—but she was also the only woman I wanted to love.

My hands gripped her luscious ass cheeks, and I kneaded them with my fingertips. My cock lay against my stomach, pulsing and anxious. I wanted to be buried inside that pussy I now called home.

She gripped my shoulders, her perfectly manicured nails pressing into my hard skin. Her face was right next to mine, but she didn't kiss me. Her beautiful and lethal expression was on me, full of arousal but so much more. This wasn't just sex to her. Her heart was practically hanging out of her chest for me to take. She'd given me her heart once, but when she took it back, it was never really out of my grasp. Now it was just guarded, wrapped in a flimsy cage.

I wished I had her heart in my palm again. I wished we were back to what we were. Someone had ripped us apart, and our love was still keeping us together—but barely.

My hand moved to the small of her back, and I tilted her forward, wanting to slide my dick inside my woman.

She moved with me, slowly taking my cock and sliding all the way down. She inched all the way to the base, taking my complete length like she was made to do it. She closed her eyes and took a deep breath, as if she couldn't believe just how good we felt together. Every time was our first time.

I gripped her hips and looked her in the eye. "Tell me to stay."

She slowly moved up until she reached my tip. Then she slid back down to my base. "Stay."

"Tell me you don't want me to be with anyone else."

She continued to ride my length, slowly dragging herself to my base before she rose up again. Her breathing was even but slowly escalating. Her nipples were hardening, dragging down my chest as they moved.

I guided her harder down my cock, exploring that soaked pussy even more.

Her lips barely touched mine as she spoke. "No one else…"

A quiet moan escaped my lips, aroused by her possessiveness, her obvious jealousy. "Tell me you love me."

She rode my length harder, taking my cock deep inside her. Her cream lubricated me all the way to the hilt. Our bodies sounded so slick together, moving past each other as we tried to claim one another entirely. She arched her back, straightened her shoulders, and tilted her chin up as she enjoyed me, as she worshiped my length with her heavenly cunt.

I sprinkled kisses along her jawline until I reached her ear. My mouth released hot breaths straight into her canal, my arousal amplified for her to hear. "Tell me." I kissed the shell of her ear and gripped both of her cheeks with my hands.

"No."

My face moved back to hers, seeing the defiance in her expression. She wasn't going to cave so easily, put all of her cards on the table. She displayed her restraint and resilience, doing her best to fight the connection that gripped us both by the throat.

Her arms circled my neck, and she fingered my hair, taking my length at an accelerated pace.

I wasn't going to let her win, no matter how good her cunt felt. She'd admitted her jealousy, her possessiveness. But I wanted more from her. I wanted to take away everything, wrap her around my finger once more.

I lifted her up and maneuvered her to her back, keeping my throbbing dick inside her. My arms widened her legs, and I conquered her with my size, making her sink into the mattress until she was nearly swallowed up by it. Her slender, lithe body couldn't make an indentation on its own. But I was nearly twice her size, over a foot taller than her, and I had more muscle in my arm than she had in her entire body.

I pounded into her, hitting her in the perfect spot over and over. I'd been with her enough times to know how to push all the right buttons. I knew exactly where her trigger was to detonate all of her explosives. I pressed deep and hard, conquering her wet pussy and making it mine. I kept my eyes on hers, wanting her to know she was mine.

Her fingers dug into my arms, and her mouth widened. The screams were about to erupt, but before she could topple over the edge and fall, I stopped. I kept my hard dick inside her, pulsing and aching. But I didn't grind my pelvic bone against her clit. I held her captive in place, on the verge of a climax that would make her legs shake. If she wanted me to please her, she had to please me first.

"Say it."

She dug her nails deeper into my skin and gave me a desperate look. She still fought me, but the battle wouldn't last long.

I pulled my dick completely out then shoved it back in, reminding her how good it felt.

She moaned right into my face.

"Tell me."

Her nipples were pointed at the ceiling, her knees were pressed into her sides, and she looked like the most succulent woman, ripe for the taking. She had my dick deep inside her, completely at my mercy. She never looked so sexy as when she had my big cock inside her. Her arms circled my neck, and her fingers clutched my hair. "I love you..."

A high unlike anything I'd felt rushed through me. It was better than landing my first business deal. It was better than when I made my first billion. I felt like I'd truly accomplished something, had done something to make me into a real man. I had the love of the most amazing woman on this planet. She could love anyone, have any man that she chose, but she only wanted me.

My hand grasped her hair, and I deepened my angle between her legs. I possessed as much of her as I could, conquering her body as well as her heart. I started to thrust into her again, giving my woman my dick the way she wanted. "I love you, baby."

## 8

WHAT THE HELL was I doing?

I woke up the next morning alone, but Hunt's scent was heavy on the sheets. Not just from last night —but also the evening before. He was between my legs when we both should have been at dinner. When it was time to go to sleep, he was still deep inside me, claiming me over and over.

After he told me he loved me, we didn't say another word to each other. Our bodies clung together like two magnets. Our writhing bodies filled the silence in the absence of conversation. He didn't tell me he loved me—he showed it.

And I was showing him the same thing.

How did I get into this mess?

It was bad enough when it happened the first night.

But a second?

Get a grip, Titan.

When I thought he went to that suite to fool around with gorgeous models, I was heartbroken. I couldn't keep a straight face in front of my colleagues, and I retreated to my room for a double shot of whiskey to calm my nerves. My eyes were wet. My palms were sweaty. My heart was aching.

And Hunt saw all of it.

He'd ambushed me, catching me when I was at my most vulnerable. He saw my feelings written across my forehead like a tattoo. My emotions were the strongest proof of my affection, that the idea of him being with someone else could move me to tears.

Damn it.

There was no point in denying it, no point in fixing my makeup. I'd told him I didn't want him anymore, but that was a bunch of bullshit. I didn't trust him anymore, but I certainly loved him as much as I ever had.

What was wrong with me?

I shouldn't let this faze me. I shouldn't let these emotions cloud my judgment. I should walk away from him like he meant nothing to me.

But I was still there, my legs wrapped around his waist with my nails digging into his back.

Pathetic.

Instead of having a cup of coffee with breakfast, I downed a drink instead. I didn't have a migraine and I'd slept like a rock, but I needed liquor to cool my nerves. I showered and got ready for the day, knowing I had a presentation with Hunt in just a few hours.

God, I had to look at his face.

His stupid, gorgeous face.

I had just slipped my heels on when there was a knock on the door.

I knew exactly who it was.

I fixed the collar of my shirt and opened the door. Hunt didn't sleep over last night or the evening before, probably because it was a dangerous move in a hotel packed with people we knew. Or maybe he just knew I wouldn't want him to stick around.

He was wrong about that.

I came face-to-face with him, seeing the eyes that looked like black coffee. His chin was shaved from his morning shower. He wore a jet-black suit that complemented his already broad shoulders and slim hips. A tight stomach led to muscled thighs and toned calves. He looked just as good dressed as he did naked.

Instead of wearing my heart on my sleeve like last night, I wore a hard mask.

His hands rested in his pockets, and he stared at

me with his usual intensity, like he owned me whether I wanted him to or not. He didn't flinch from my gaze, powerful and exuding strength.

I kept one hand on the door, my back perfectly straight and my shoulders back. I looked at him like last night never happened, like he was just a colleague that didn't mean a damn thing to me.

"Let's work on our presentation."

My walls slowly came down when I realized this was purely a business meeting. I wasn't about to let my clothes come off this early in the morning. I stepped away from the entryway and left the door open.

Hunt followed me inside and took a seat on one of the couches in the sitting area. I had a full living room with a great view of the water. Sunlight sprinkled the horizon, and the boats in the harbor were glowing. He crossed one leg and rested his ankle on the opposite knee. It was exactly how he always sat whenever he did business. If it was just the two of us in my penthouse, he took up more space than necessary.

I grabbed my laptop and took a seat on the couch across from him, pretending last night never happened. Now we were two partners who only cared about business. I opened up the presentation on the screen then glanced up at him.

His eyes were on my nearly empty glass. He flicked

them back to me and didn't seem to care that I caught him staring. He rested one hand on his knee while the other arm draped over the back of the couch. "Little early to drink, isn't it?"

"A little early to judge, isn't it?"

His expression remained as hard as it had been by the door. "No judgment. Just concern."

"I don't need your concern, Hunt."

His eyes narrowed. "I thought we weren't playing games anymore, Titan."

"I'm not."

"Then don't say you don't need me when we both know you do."

I held his gaze without blinking, put off by the romantic comment. When he'd arrived at my door, he seemed professional. I thought we could skip the conversation about us and get right to work. "I'm only interested in work right now, Hunt."

"As am I. That means my partner shouldn't be drunk."

I kept my voice steady even though I felt my anger rising. "I'm not drunk."

"If you drink at nine, then yes, you're a goddamn drunk."

If my laptop weren't precious to me, I would have thrown it at his face. "If I were a man, you wouldn't think twice about my consumption. You wouldn't question my ability to complete the task at hand."

"You being a woman has nothing to do with it. It has nothing to do with work either. I have a very personal investment in you, Titan. And when you drink like that, I worry. Don't make me worry."

"Trust me, I don't want to." I turned back to my laptop, silently dismissing the conversation. "How do you want to do this? Should you go first, or should I?"

He adjusted his tie. "Ladies first."

Now my eyes burned through his suit. "We're business partners. We're equals. Don't pull that chivalry bullshit. It doesn't apply here." I wanted to be treated as one of the men. I didn't need my partner to be a gentleman just because of what was between my legs.

He didn't hide the smirk creeping onto his lips. "Fine. I should lead."

I felt the irritation move into my skin, hating the fact that I had to share the stage with someone. I was used to doing everything on my own. I did what I wanted without answering to anyone.

His smile grew wider. "Do you want to go first?"

"Of course I do."

He couldn't suppress his chuckle. "Then go first."

"Do you think that would be best for the presentation?"

"You're great at public speaking, as am I. But you're far more entertaining to look at."

I couldn't suppress my scoff. "All the women here would say otherwise."

"Well, there's only five of them. They're outnumbered."

"But not in intensity."

He hadn't dropped his smile so far in this conversation. "Well, we both know how jealous you get..."

I absorbed the jab while keeping my face a mask. There wasn't a smartass comment I could make to get me out of that. I'd walked into my hotel room on the verge of tears. He saw the whole thing. It was burned into the backs of his eyelids, seared into his memory. "Like you're any better." When Marshall Tucker stared at me a little too long, Hunt didn't hesitate before he chewed his head off.

Hunt smiled wider. "I'm a very jealous man when it comes to my woman."

---

WE WERE SCHEDULED TO SPEAK FOR FIFTEEN MINUTES, but it felt like less than five. Hunt was a natural when all eyes were on him. He was just as calm and suave as ever. And he had the audacity to give me that exact stare he gave me behind closed doors.

Because he was arrogant like that.

After a round of applause, the audience fired off questions. Unlike when I took the stage on my own, not a single sexist comment was fired our way. No one seemed to care about my age, my lack of children, or how tight my skirt was.

I suspected that had something to do with Hunt.

The moment we were off the stage and out of the spotlight, I felt a little better. Any time I was the center of attention, walls as thick as a stadium surrounded me. I anticipated the cold insults and veiled jabs. I expected to work three times as hard to be taken as seriously as a man. If I were an average woman, no one would question anything about me. But as a successful entrepreneur, my professionalism was constantly categorized as bossy or bitchy. I had to wear a smile when most men would wear a frown. I had to be perfectly manicured. Otherwise, I would be called a hag. But if a man showed up in jeans and a t-shirt covered in stains, people would laugh it off and call him ballsy.

And I would be labeled a pig.

Most of the time, those kinds of double standards didn't penetrate my rock-hard exterior. But I couldn't deny the reasons behind my layers. I was prepared for the harshness of my reality at all times. So once I was out of the spotlight, I felt like a human being again— not a human target.

Hunt appeared beside me, and his hand rested on the small of my back.

To anyone else, the touch could be considered professional affection between two colleagues.

I knew it was nothing but possessiveness on his part.

He guided me out of the conference room into the main lobby, where snacks and beverages were served. In just a few minutes, we would be swarmed with people who hadn't had a chance to ask their questions at the end of the presentation.

"That went well."

I kept my eyes forward, smiling at people who gave me a nod in greeting. "I think so too."

"You did great."

"Thanks. You did too."

"Well, I always do great."

When I looked up at him, I saw the smile on his face.

"I did even better than usual because you were the one standing up there with me." He dropped his hand from my back and grabbed two glasses of water. He handed me one as he held the other.

I stared at it blankly, unsure why he thought I would have any interest in it.

He leaned toward me and brought his mouth dangerously close to my ear. "Drink it. Or I'll kiss you."

My eyes widened as I stared at him.

"Call my bluff." He took a sip from his glass. "I dare you."

I knew Hunt wasn't toying with me. He would take any excuse he could get to kiss me in a room full of people. He didn't like being a secret when we were together, and even now when we were apart, he still didn't want to be a secret.

So I drank.

"Good girl."

I lowered my glass and prepared to throw the water in his face. "Don't call me that. Makes me sound like a dog."

He returned his hand to the small of my back. "Alright."

It was rare that Hunt listened to what I said without making a smartass comment, so I knew he took my words seriously. I took another drink of my water even though I was craving something else— something stronger.

"I'm having dinner with a few guys tonight. You wanna come along?"

"I'll make my own dinner plans."

He brought me closer into his side and lowered his face to mine. "That wasn't a pity invite. I want you there."

"I knew it wasn't a pity invite. I'm definitely not a person you should pity."

"Not when you're hot as fire and hard as ice." He set his glass down on the table before he placed his hand in his pocket. His hand stayed on my lower back, never leaving. "There's a few people I want you to meet. One is a professional golfer."

"I do love to golf."

"And the other is the biggest cosmetics owner in all of China. I think you two will have a lot to talk about."

I knew exactly who he was referring to. I knew everyone in my own space. "Kyle Livingston?"

"Yeah."

"I didn't know he was here."

"It's a good thing you got a pity invite, then, huh?" he teased.

"Who's the golfer?"

"Rick Perry."

He was one of the biggest stars of the sport. He

started right out of high school, made it to the pros, and now he was leading the field. "How do you know him?"

He winked. "Baby, I know everyone."

"Don't call me that in public."

"Fine." He slowly pulled his hand away from my waist. "I'll save that for tonight."

---

EVEN MY COMPLICATED SITUATION WITH HUNT wouldn't stop me from attending that dinner. China was a market I'd been trying to get into for years, but due to international complications, it hadn't been as easy as I wanted it to be. There was a lot of competition from Kyle's company, which had shelves in nearly every single store. He didn't have the prominence that I did in the U. S, which was the bigger market. We could both use each other—if we played our cards right.

But I was also interested in Rick Perry. I'd been playing golf for a long time. It was a slow sport, but it was much more complicated than people assumed. Having meetings on the links wasn't always so easy because my concentration was split into two different directions.

I sat beside Rick with Hunt on my left. His legs stretched out under the table, tapping against my knee —on purpose. He looked for any excuse to touch me, any way to get under my skin.

Rick was young, in his late twenties. He had sun-kissed skin, a great smile, and his slender build looked great in a t-shirt. He had slim hips and broad shoulders the way I liked. His physique didn't compare to Hunt's, which was packed with muscle and arrogance.

"I saw you at Pebble Beach last year for the Champions Tour." I went to California often, and not just because I had a home in San Diego. I did a lot of work in the Monterey Peninsula. Lots of business owners had settled there to get away from the sweltering heat of Manhattan. "You're a great golfer."

Rick's face lit up with a smile like my compliment actually meant something to him. "Thanks. You follow golf?"

"Yeah. And I play a lot."

"Really?" Kyle Livingston cocked his head to the side and examined me like I was a freak.

The feminist inside me always wanted to rise to these outbursts of surprise. Men were perpetually surprised to hear I had a collection of racing cars and autographed baseballs. Apparently, sports and women didn't mix—which was ridiculous. "Yes. It's a pastime I enjoy." I kept the annoyance out of my voice, knowing his opinion didn't truly matter. Our relationship was only based on business. I didn't get tied up in the personal stuff.

"Are you any good?" Kyle crossed his arms over his chest, still looking at me like I'd sprouted a second head.

Hunt was silent beside me, knowing I could handle these conversations like all the others.

"Care to find out?" I challenged.

Rick chuckled. "I'd like to find out. They have a great course here just five miles from shore. Are you free tomorrow?"

"Titan and I are heading back home in the morning." Hunt had stopped eating his food, no longer interested in the green salad he ordered. He usually ordered a beer when he was out in public, but he stuck to water again tonight—like it was just for me.

I had a private plane, so I left whenever I felt like it. It was obvious Hunt was just trying to keep Rick away from me because he assumed the golfer was interested in me. But Hunt was paranoid and assumed every straight man wanted me—which they didn't.

Rick didn't challenge Hunt's statement. "That's too bad. When I'm in New York, I'll set up something. I should be there in a few weeks anyway."

Hunt clenched his jaw but didn't make a comment about it.

"Great." I pulled out my business card and set it on the table. "Give me a call."

Hunt looked like he wanted to snatch it.

Rick dropped it into a slot in his wallet. "Awesome. Never thought I'd play golf with Tatum Titan."

"And lose to Tatum Titan," I teased.

"Ooh..." Rick chuckled. "Wow. I've got a real competitor on my hands." He had a charming smile that seemed genuine. Unlike most professional athletes I met, who were too arrogant to really care about a conversation, Rick Perry seemed different. He seemed like a person more than an athlete.

Kyle finally dropped the discussion about my golfing abilities. "I liked your presentation back there, but I noticed there was no mention of your Illuminance line."

"Hunt and I only work together for Stratosphere." Hunt and I never exchanged conversations about our various businesses. Everything else seemed like a conflict of interest since some of our businesses were in competition with one another, at least peripherally. We both had our own approaches to investments. I wasn't going to give away my secrets to him, and I would judge him if he gave me his.

"Must be hard to keep things separate," Kyle asked. "Since you work together all the time."

"Not at all," Hunt said. "Lots of business owners do business with other people. It's not groundbreaking by any means."

"I have a confession to make," Kyle said as he looked at me. "My wife prefers the foundation from Illuminance over mine. She says it's not so oily and complements her skin tone a lot better."

Since it was phrased as a compliment, I took it that way. "Thank you. All of our products are organic. More compatible with the pH of the skin as well as the oils."

"Depends on the person," Kyle said. "But I see your point. I've been wanting to branch into the American market. But honestly, it's pretty tough with your line on every shelf."

Even though my heart began to race, I kept a professional smile. It was obvious Kyle and I had the exact same desires. He needed me to get into the high-end retailers, and I needed him to get into the right marketplaces in China. It could be a mutually beneficial relationship if we allowed it to be done. "It's pretty tough to enter China when you're overwhelming all the stores."

"Kyle, you'd be lucky to have a business partner

like Titan," Hunt said. "She's the only person I've ever worked with—for a reason."

I couldn't look at him without making it obvious his words meant something to me. He purposely arranged this meeting so I could sit down with Kyle. There was no way it was a coincidence. He was trying to push me forward, to get me to go further.

"That's saying something," Rick said. "Hunt is a picky guy."

"The pickiest guy," Hunt said. "But Titan's business expertise puts her above the rest. Not only can you trust her work, but her loyalty. She won't let you down." His arm moved to the back of my chair, a possessive gesture that most people wouldn't pick up on.

Kyle wore a guarded expression just the way I did. He wasn't as high on the *Forbes* list as Hunt and me, but he still possessed considerable wealth and connections. After a long stare-down, he spoke to me. "How about we set up a meeting when we return to New York? My assistant will make the arrangements with yours?"

I was just given a key piece to my puzzle. Now I could expand even further, bring my luxury product into more hands who wanted it. "I think that sounds like a great idea."

BUSINESS TURNED INTO SPORTS, AND SPORTS TURNED into women. They didn't hold back just because I was there, and that was something I appreciated. Most of my colleagues were men, and all men were the same. They thought with their brain when it came to money, but when it came to women, they thought with a different piece of their anatomy.

"What about you, Hunt?" Kyle asked. "Last I heard, you were with some blonde outside of that club."

I didn't want to hear this conversation. I did a great job pretending not to care where Hunt slept every night, but listening to him talk about the women he'd been with wasn't entertaining to me. Even if he had to lie about it, I still didn't like the images he painted. I never thought of myself as a jealous person, but being with Hunt made me realize I wasn't so easygoing. All of my other partners hadn't made a dent in my possessiveness. But Hunt created a huge hole right through me.

"Don't believe everything in the tabloids," Hunt said coolly. "That woman was drunk off her ass, so I gave her a ride home."

"Bullshit," Rick said. "We know you're the biggest playboy in Manhattan."

I wanted to cover my ears. The last thing I wanted to hear was another blow job story.

Hunt didn't say anything. Instead, he covered his silence with a drink.

"Come on," Kyle said. "Who is she? What nasty shit have you gotten yourself into?"

"I don't kiss and tell," Hunt said. "I'm a gentleman."

"You weren't a gentleman New Year's Eve last year," Kyle jabbed.

I knew Hunt was being quiet for my sake, and I appreciated it. I didn't want to hear a single tale about a threesome or a foursome. "It's getting late, gentlemen." I rose from my chair with the same charismatic smile I had plastered on my face fifteen minutes ago. "I'm sure you have a lot to talk about—"

"I'm seeing someone," Hunt blurted without looking at me. "And I'm in love with her."

Oh god.

He didn't say that, did he?

"What?" Rick asked incredulously. "You? In love? With who?"

"Yeah," Kyle asked. "Who are you talking about?"

I had to get out of there. "Good night. Have a safe trip back everyone." I turned away from the table, but the men didn't care I was leaving.

They were more interested in Hunt's announcement.

"Who is it?" Kyle pressed. "Is she an actress?"

Hunt retained his composure. "She's pretty well-known. She wants to keep our relationship a secret for a while so it won't be a feast for the paparazzi." He rose from his chair. "I'll be right back. I'm just gonna walk Titan to her room."

"I don't need to be walked," I blurted, flustered by the sudden change in atmosphere for the evening.

Hunt moved his arm to the small of my back and escorted me out of the restaurant until we were out of sight.

"What the hell are you doing?" I rounded on him and struggled to keep my voice down. Luckily, no one was in the hallway.

"I'm tired of lying, Titan." His expression mixed with remorse as well as a lack of contrition. "I don't want to do it anymore."

"We aren't together anymore, Hunt. So you don't need to lie."

"We are together," he said quietly. "We were together last night, the night before, and you bet your ass, we'll be together tonight."

My palm seared with heat as I ached to slap him. "It was meaningless sex."

He shook his head slightly. "How many times did you tell me you loved me last night? Five times?"

"Only because you made me."

He chuckled sarcastically. "No one makes Tatum Titan do anything—and you know it."

His gorgeous features and devastatingly beautiful eyes couldn't chase away my wrath this time. I was losing control, and everything was starting to spin. I didn't like it one bit. "Knock it off, Hunt. This is a secret—and it'll stay a secret."

"I don't want to be a dirty secret anymore."

"Then you shouldn't have stabbed me in the back," I hissed. "You shouldn't have betrayed me. You shouldn't have fucked that—"

"You know I didn't do it. Your heart and your brain are at war with each other right now, but if you looked past that, you would know how you really feel. You wouldn't have ridden me bareback last night if you thought I was getting my dick wet in other places. The only woman I've been plowing for six months is you." He stuck his finger in my face. "Just you."

I shoved his hand out of my face. "You promised me you would keep this between us. Are you going to break that promise too?"

His jaw tightened, and he squared his shoulders. "I'm only obligated to keep your identity a secret. But

I'm not obligated to lie about loving you, about being committed to another person. I'm tired of pretending to be America's playboy when I've found my future wife. I'm sick of it, Titan. I want to grab your face and kiss you in front of everyone in that goddamn room and just get it over with. I want every man to know I'm the one fucking you every night, not Thorn Cutler."

My rage diminished as his words swept over me. There was so much hostility but so much sweetness in his comeback. I'd have to be made of stone not to be affected by it. I would have to be heartless not to feel weak in the knees. I'd thought about my future with Hunt many times, and every single version ended with me in a white dress with a diamond ring on my finger. I loved this man with all my heart—and he knew it. "Go back in there and continue your conversation."

"I'd rather be with you."

"Well, you aren't going to be with me." I walked past him, my shoulder brushing his.

He grabbed my wrist and turned me around. "Titan—"

"Don't come to my room tonight. I mean it."

He kept his grip on my wrist, but his eyes were what squeezed me.

"This has to stop. It's not going anywhere. We're just—"

"Two people in love," he whispered. "Two people who should be together."

"I don't trust you." I didn't know what to think. He told me he didn't announce his sexual conquests, but he obviously did. He'd told me he just took that woman home, but I saw him kiss her. He told me he didn't sell me out, but all the evidence pointed to him. But I couldn't shake this feeling in my heart. "Just leave me alone, Hunt."

He yanked me closer to him before he fished out his wallet.

I watched him dig it out of his trousers and open the billfold, having no idea what he was doing.

He took out the white keycard to his room and held it up. "I won't come to your room tonight. But I know you'll come to mine." He slipped it underneath the fabric of my dress and directly into one of the cups of my bra. "I'm calling your bluff, Titan." He shoved his wallet back into his back pocket and walked away. "And I'll always call your bluff."

---

I wasn't going to his room.

Forget it.

I washed off my makeup just to prove it to myself. I changed out of my clothes and pulled on a nightdress.

I was staying put.

I worked on my computer for a few hours, answering the emails that surged after my presentation. Jessica had a few documents for me to sign electronically, and I got quarterly numbers for a few of my smaller businesses.

The time ticked away.

A few hours later, I glanced at the clock and realized it was almost midnight.

I should get some sleep.

I shut my laptop then got into bed, the entire mattress for me to enjoy. The sheets were cool to the touch, and the room was dead silent. I couldn't even hear the AC unit. It was the perfect conditions to slip away into slumber.

But my thoughts turned back to Hunt.

He was in his room waiting for me. He said I would come to him, but I couldn't fulfill his prediction. I couldn't prove him right.

My thighs ached to grip his waist, and I felt the shivers move up my spine from the cold. When he was in this bed with me, naked and muscular, he seared the sheets with his warm body. He worked up a sweat and rubbed the drops against my skin. Our heart rates escalated, and our temperatures soared. It was so hot it was unbearable, but it made sleeping that much easier.

I would love to have that beautiful man between my legs.

But I wasn't going to do it.

No.

My phone sat on the nightstand along with the keycard he'd slipped into my bra. The room number was written on the top corner, and I realized it was right next door to mine.

I was sure he'd arranged that.

I closed my eyes and faced the ceiling, clearing my thoughts of Hunt and focusing on the stars in the sky. I tried to picture how the heavens looked this evening, but my mind kept slipping away to dirtier things.

Hunt plowing himself deep inside me.

Telling me I was beautiful.

Breathing into my mouth as he kissed me.

Palming my tits with his big hands.

Making me come over and over.

I changed positions on the bed, tossing and turning. But the train of my thoughts couldn't be derailed, and my skin turned warmer. My hand wanted to move between my legs, but that would be a weak release. It would be so much better with a real man pleasing me, his muscular physique forcing me to sink into the sheets.

God, I wanted him.

And I hated him so much for that.

It was a stupid decision, but I was so anxious I didn't think logically anymore. Now I only wanted one thing, and I wasn't going to stop until I got it. Hunt called my bluff, but he was the kind of guy who wouldn't gloat.

I changed and grabbed the keycard before I walked out.

His door was just fifteen feet down the hallway. No one was in the hallway, thankfully. If someone spotted me, I'd have to make up an excuse to explain why I was walking around the hotel at midnight without any makeup on.

I reached his door and hesitated before I inserted the card. I didn't know if he would be sitting on the couch waiting for me, or if he would be buck naked the second I stepped inside. He slept in the nude, so I wouldn't be surprised if that's what I was greeted with.

At least, I hoped it was.

I opened the door and stepped inside his dark room. All the lights were out. Only the gentle glow from the hallway illuminated the floor in front of me. Maybe he assumed I wasn't coming, so he went to bed.

A tall silhouette appeared and walked toward me, heavy footfalls that echoed against the floor with every step he took. He came closer, his physique and expression more visible as he drew near. Over six feet of impressive muscle, he was a beast as well as a man.

His eyes came into view, and they were glued to mine, fiery and terrifying. He was the only man in the world who could make me second-guess myself, to intimidate me with just his appearance. If ever I felt threatened by someone, I gave them a reason to feel threatened by me. But that didn't work with Hunt. He was far too confident, far too powerful to feel such an inferior emotion. The harder I became, the more I straightened, the more he wanted me. He was the kind of man who didn't feel emasculated by a woman's success. Instead, it was a turn-on.

I didn't step back as he crowded me, and when he was closer, I realized he was buck naked—like I'd hoped he'd be. With a powerful chest, broad shoulders, and tight arms, he was a powerhouse of muscular strength. I looked up into his face, seeing the same aggression he wore at dinner.

His hands yanked my dress over my head with a lack of gentleness. He practically ripped the fabric, stretching out the expensive dress that Connor had given to me. I was commando when I came over, so there were no panties to discard. He glanced between my legs, the arousal starting to boil in his eyes. He snapped my bra off before he crushed his mouth against mine, taking me roughly without an introduction.

His powerful hands gripped me and kept me rigidly in place so he could have as much of me as he wanted. He squeezed me hard and gave me his tongue, bringing our heat to a peak instantly. He sucked on my bottom lip, breathed into my mouth, and then jerked me into his arms before he carried me to the bed.

He dropped me on the sheets then pinned both of my wrists above my head. He held himself on top of me, two hundred pounds of heavy muscle that immediately brought me warmth. His dark eyes resembled chocolate, and I wanted them to melt all over my skin. Without breaking eye contact, he wrapped a thick piece of rope around my wrists and secured my arms to the headboard.

"What are you—"

He pressed his mouth to mine and silenced my words with his tongue.

I yanked on the rope and felt the tightness. There was no wiggle room at all. Even with a knife, I'd have a hard time getting out of this.

He ended the embrace and pinned my knees

directly against my waist. "You walked into my territory. Now we play by my rules." He wrapped the rope around my body in intricate ways, positioning my legs in place so I was completely open to him. He'd never tied me this way, left me completely impaired and at his mercy.

"Hunt—"

He positioned his face between my legs, where I would be fully exposed and vulnerable to his mouth. He kissed my tender folds and dragged his tongue across my sex, tasting me and exploring me.

The words died on my tongue, and I released an unrestrained moan.

Hunt positioned his big hands under my thighs and gripped the area as he continued to feast on me, enjoy me as much as he wanted. His tongue explored my aching slit before it circled my throbbing clit.

I closed my eyes and breathed through the pleasure, feeling Hunt give me a fantasy I hadn't realized I had. He pleased me exactly the way I wanted to be pleased. He made me feel so good, made me forget about everything else in the world besides his mouth.

Just before he brought me to a powerful climax, he pulled his mouth away and climbed on top of me.

"Diesel..." I wasn't above begging at this point. I'd been wrestling with my desire for the past few hours. I wanted him to please me in the fantastic way he'd been doing for months. I opened my eyes and looked into his dark expression.

He pressed his length against my soaked folds and slowly ground against me, watching my face the entire time. His scorching expression didn't change as he pressed his cock hard against me, giving me the kind of friction that would make my legs shake if they could move.

He lowered his head farther until our faces were nearly touching.

I tried to grind against him, but when I moved, he stopped. "Diesel."

"You've been torturing me for weeks now. My turn to torture you." He ground against me again, his pulsing cock pressing right against my clit.

My hands yanked toward him, and then I was reminded that thick ropes kept me in place. I couldn't move a single part of my body besides my head. I was completely at his mercy, this powerful man conquering me like a country being overtaken.

He pressed his face to mine and kissed me, giving me a slow embrace that was contradictory to the way he greeted me by the door. It was soft and sensual, full of restrained urgency. Even when I kissed him harder, he wouldn't pick up his pace. He took the control back every time I tried to hijack it.

"Diesel." I spoke against his mouth as he continued to kiss me and grind his cock against me. "Fuck me."

He took a deep breath, as if my words burned all the way down his spine. "I haven't decided how I'm going to fuck you—in the cunt or the ass."

I forgot to breathe when I heard his words, my entire body flushing with heat. "I want to feel your come in my pussy."

He stopped grinding against me, his eyes flashing. "I don't care what you want."

I took a deep breath, pressing my nipples toward the ceiling. "Then pick, Diesel. Just fuck me already." I yanked on the ropes even though I would never break free. I didn't like being told what to do, being tied up and unable to move. Being powerless was a hard limit for me, but with Hunt, I didn't feel insecure. I wasn't scared. It felt right—like I was in the safest place in the world.

With his teeth pressed against my jaw, he growled. It was menacing and guttural, terrifying and territorial. He tilted his hips back then pressed the head of his fat cock inside me. My slick entrance made it easy for him slide all the way through until he reached my cervix. He was thick and long, and it was like my pussy had never taken him before.

I took another deep breath even though my lungs didn't have the room.

"Fuck." He positioned himself on top of me, looking straight down into my face. His aerial view allowed him to see all of me, studying the way I was vulnerable with my knees secured to my waist. My nipples were pebbling, and my chest flushed a bright pink color. He let his massive cock sit inside me like he was getting reacquainted with my body after spending only a day apart. "You're all mine, Titan." He started to thrust inside me, a perfect pace that wasn't slow or fast. His strokes were even and deep, guaranteed to bring me to climax in less than a minute.

He delivered, and I felt the explosion between my legs, the powerful sensation I'd been craving all night. It was searing hot and so satisfying, strong enough to make me feel crippled when it was over. It was the kind of orgasm no other man could give me. My hand certainly couldn't do it either. I turned into a puddle of goo, only feeling and not thinking. "Thank you..." I didn't think twice before the words slipped from my mouth. When Hunt was buried between my legs, I could barely form coherent sentences.

"Don't thank me for doing my job, baby." He

pressed his mouth to mine and gave me a tender kiss, the kind he usually gave when sex was over. It was all lips and no tongue, but it was just as sensual. He kissed the corner of my mouth then dragged his teeth across my jaw. "How many times do you want to come tonight?"

"I thought you were in charge."

"I am." He spoke against my ear. "Which is why I'm the one asking the questions."

Despite being with him last night and the night before, I was so desperate for him it was like I hadn't had sex in years. It felt like I hadn't had a beautiful, sweaty man on top of me in ages. I rocked my body back into him with the limited mobility that I had, breathing and moaning as I sheathed his dick with my cream over and over.

"How many?" he whispered.

"As many as you can give me."

He pressed his mouth over my ear as his hand fisted my hair. "Alright, then."

---

WE LAY IN THE DARK TOGETHER, HIS CHEST PRESSED against my back. Hours had passed, and neither one of us could continue anymore. My body was sore from his enormous dick, and my skin had marks from where the ropes had cut into me. His face was pressed into the back of my neck, and his steady breaths floated across my skin. His muscular arm was wrapped around my waist, holding me tightly like I might slip away.

It would be so easy to stay here, to sleep the entire night with this sexy man pressed right against me. I loved the way his chest expanded into my back every time he took a breath. I loved the way he smelled, masculine mixed with a hint of mint. I missed this comfort. I used to hate sleeping beside him. It was too hard. But now that I'd stopped sleeping with him, my nights were restless. I was tired all the time because I'd turned into an insomniac.

So I wanted to stay—right there.

But I couldn't do that. Sleeping with him three nights in a row was bad enough. It made our complicated situation even more tangled. My desires were unclear—even to me. I didn't know what I wanted, and I didn't know how to stop myself from this addiction. I wanted to move on and forget about him, but I was in so deep it was hard to get out. But if I slept beside him all night, cuddled up together as a single person, it would put me even deeper into the hole.

And I might never get out.

I slowly slid from his grasp toward the edge of the bed. If I was quiet enough, he might not feel me slip away. Once he knew I was retreating, he would grab me and yank me back into bed, his arms acting as bars of a cell.

I reached the end but didn't get far.

His large hand grabbed me by the wrist and yanked me back against his chest. It was like crashing into a mountain. I was shaken, but he remained solid. "No." Like a caveman who only knew a few words, he said it as a command.

"I'm tired."

"Then lie still and go to sleep."

"You know I don't want to sleep with you." I moved away from him.

He yanked me back. "How many times am I going to call your bluff in a single day?" He positioned me in front of him and locked his arm around my waist so I couldn't crawl away again. "You came to my lair tonight. My rules."

It would easy to give up and just enjoy it. But I couldn't allow that to happen. "We don't sleep together." I pushed his arm off. "I'm not changing my mind."

This time, he let me go, his heavy arm moving to the side like a gate.

I rose to my feet and pulled my clothes from the floor.

He propped himself up on his elbow, looking at me with obvious irritation. He could push me, but there were times when I refused to be pushed. Right now, he knew my decision was as solid as concrete. "We have to talk about this when we get back."

"Nothing to talk about." I couldn't look at him, not when he was naked in bed with the sheets bunched around his waist, the shape of his semihard dick outlined by the soft fabric. His hair was ruffled from my fingertips, and his sleepy expression was undeniably sexy. He was the most desirable man in the world, and I could have him a little longer if I stayed in that bed. But I couldn't have a man I didn't trust. Trust was everything to me—and we didn't have it.

"We'll see." He lay down again with his eyes on the ceiling. "When is your plane leaving?"

"I'll probably leave after I shower—sleep on the plane."

"Then I'll see you around, Titan." He got comfortable and closed his eyes. "Don't forget to leave some money on the table. You know, because I'm your whore." Without raising his voice or even changing his tone, he announced his rage. He rested his hand behind his head while the other rested on his chest.

I pulled on my clothes and remained by the bed, feeling the wound from the invisible knife. He made me feel guilty when I had nothing to feel guilty about. He was the untruthful one, the untrustworthy one. I was still playing this game while keeping my heart out of the ring—at least, most of it. But he tore at my armor, hit me in a weak spot I didn't detect. He knew exactly how I felt about him, so the insult was just a jab to get a rise out of me. He'd say anything to get me back in that bed.

I hated to admit it was working.

I crawled back on the bed and held myself above his face.

He opened his eyes when he knew I was there. His eyes were deep brown like the earth, full of life and vitality. He was well-read, so every expression he made told a story. I could see his emotions at all times. He didn't need to speak for me to know if he was angry, sad, or simply affectionate.

I leaned down and kissed him on the mouth, keeping it subtle and soft. If tongue got involved, I'd be back in that bed with my bra thrown across the room. I felt the stubble around his mouth with my soft lips and felt him breathe in when he felt me. "I love you."

He smiled against my mouth and dug his hand into my hair. He deepened the kiss and breathed with me, his affection masculine and soothing. "And I love you, baby. So fucking much."

---

I SLEPT ON THE PLANE AND GOT BACK TO WORK THE NEXT morning. Even taking a few days off put me behind. Work never slept, and sometimes I wished I didn't need to sleep either. I stayed at my main office near my penthouse and skipped Stratosphere since that's all I'd been focusing on over the weekend.

I hadn't spoken to Hunt since I'd left his room. Having some space away from would do me some good. Whenever we were in the same room together, clothes always came off and our bodies combined together. It was a terrible sickness I couldn't overcome. When we were apart, it was a lot easier for me to be pragmatic.

Jessica's voice came over the intercom. "Mr. Hunt is here to see you."

Goddammit. "Why?"

"I...I don't know. I just thought it was okay if he didn't have an appointment. Do you want me to tell him to leave?"

I sighed before I returned my finger to the button. "No. Send him in."

"Yes, Titan."

A moment later, Jessica opened the glass doors and ushered Hunt inside. He looked sexy naked with messy hair, but when he was dressed up in a fresh suit with his hair styled, he looked even more scrumptious. He walked into my office like he owned the space and took a seat in the chair facing my desk. I wasn't greeted with a hello, not even a smile. I just got his intense expression, his bedroom eyes. He never cared if anyone noticed the way he stared at me. He would do it even with a camera pointed in his face.

"What can I do for you?" I asked as I looked back at my computer screen. My glass doors allowed my assistants to look inside my office. I had nothing hide and didn't need privacy. Jessica could see when I was on the phone so, she knew not to bother me with a message. Once the phone was on the receiver, she made her move. Made the day a lot more productive.

"It's time for that conversation." He rested his ankle on the opposite knee and took up most of the chair, his sculpted physique blocking most of the chair from view. His navy blue suit was a great complement to his tanned skin and dark hair. But then again, he could wear an orange suit and still look impeccable.

"What conversation?"

He cocked his head slightly to the side. "You know what conversation I'm talking about."

It was a conversation I didn't want to have at all, let alone in my office. "Not during business hours."

"I'm just as busy as you, and I managed to squeeze it into my schedule." He winked. "You're a priority."

"Well, you aren't a priority of mine."

He grinned. "Until the lights are out and the sun is gone…"

I turned back to my computer, refusing to let him see the effect he had on me.

"So, I've been thinking a lot about it. I'd like to reopen our previous arrangement."

My eyes turned back to him because I couldn't pretend to be interested in my emails anymore.

When he had my attention, his eyes narrowed. "We both know the sex is going to keep happening. Let's not waste time denying it. Well, *you* shouldn't waste time denying it. But I'd like to have ground rules so we know exactly where the other stands. In your gut, you know I didn't do any of the things I'm accused of. Your brain can't reconcile with your heart, and that's fine with me. I'll be patient because you're worth waiting for. So this arrangement will do for now."

What I wanted to embark on was a longstanding arrangement with Hunt. Lots of good sex without the romance. It was easier that way. If we returned to that, I could have all the fun without the risk. "How will this work?"

"We take turns. Neither one of us is permanently in charge."

"And how will we decide that?"

He tapped his fingers against the wood of the armrest. "We'll know at the time. There are times when you want to be fucked out of your mind. There are times when I enjoy being slapped around...we'll play it by ear."

The rules would be far less rigid now. It wasn't how I preferred to operate. "I'm in control at all times. After all, you did betray me."

He shook his head slightly. "It's an even divide of power. Or no arrangement at all. Those are my terms."

"What makes you think you get to have terms at all?" I challenged.

He narrowed his dark eyes on my face. "Because I've been nothing but loyal to you since the day we met. You'll see it...eventually."

I doubted I would ever get any concrete proof. Even now, I still wasn't sure what to think. Hunt was a smart man. It would be easy for him to manipulate me now that he knew me so well. But my heart ached so deeply for him. If I weren't so in love with him, I'd turn my back so hard. The only reason I was interested in this arrangement was because I knew I couldn't walk away from him—not yet.

"Equal share of power," he said. "Do you agree?"

I knew Hunt wasn't wearing a poker face. He wouldn't compromise on his end of the bargain. "Yes."

"Good. We're monogamous. We're equals. And this arrangement has no deadline."

"Fine."

"Excellent." He stood up and buttoned the front of his suit, never taking his eyes off me. "You know I didn't do it, Titan."

I held his gaze and didn't blink.

He lowered his hands to his sides and stared at me with the same intensity. "Ignore the so-called facts. Go with your gut. When has your gut ever been wrong?"

"Once." And it was the biggest mistake I'd ever made. It nearly cost me my life. It could have put Thorn in prison for murder. It cost me years of heartbreak and stress. "And I still regret it to this day."

"I'm not going to be a regret, Titan." He spoke with the same tone and forcefulness, but he seemed softer. His eyes lost their rigid coldness, and he gave me an affectionate look he only showed when we were alone together. "You know I love you. You know I would never hurt you. Everything is stacked up against me, but that doesn't mean anything."

"The evidence is pretty damning."

"But my word means more. I'll do everything I can to exonerate myself. But if I can't, you need to believe me. You need to trust me."

"I don't think I can..."

"Yes, you can. Why am I in your bed every night?"

I refused to look away even though I didn't want to hold the contact any longer.

"If you believed I did any of those things, you wouldn't let me touch you. But you tell me you love me while I'm buried between your legs every night. You kiss me like I'm the only man you've ever loved."

I blinked first, troubled by what he said.

He leaned forward and rested his hands on the desk, casting a shadow across the entire room. "You believe me. I know you do. You just don't know it yet."

---

THE ELEVATOR BEEPED BEFORE THE DOORS OPENED.

Now that Hunt and I had started our new arrangement, I wasn't sure if he was the one stopping by or Thorn. It could be either man.

But it was Thorn. He was in a t-shirt and jeans,

telling me that he'd hit the gym then showered before he stopped by. He didn't make public appearances dressed in anything but his finest attire. Only behind closed doors and with trusted friends did he drop his suit and adopt his casualness. "Hey."

I was sitting on the couch with my laptop resting on my thighs. "Hey."

He went to the kitchen and helped himself to a glass of water. "Got any dinner?"

"Leftovers are in the fridge."

He riffled around in the background, popped a plate in the microwave, and then took a seat at the kitchen table. He had his own butler to cook for him, but he raided my fridge several times a week.

I joined him at the table with my own glass of water.

Thorn scooped the food into his mouth with his fork, his eyes on his plate.

"Skip lunch today?"

"I had a lot of meetings, and they only had muffins. Can't eat that shit."

"You can indulge once in a while."

"You're one to talk."

I hardly ate anything so I could continue to fit into my dresses and skirts. Once I hit thirty, my metabolism had slowed down. I had to eat even less just to keep my waistline the same. "How was work?"

"Good. I'm expanding the business and opening a new plant in the Midwest. In a small town with lots of land. It'll give jobs to the population, so it'll be easy to get all the permits. How was France?"

"Beautiful, like always."

"We should go for our honeymoon."

The mention of our marriage made me think of Hunt, who wasn't going to let me go without a fight. "Maybe. Kind of a high-profile place."

"That's the point." He scooped another bite into his mouth. "How was the conference? Did Hunt give you any trouble?"

Normally, I would tell Thorn exactly what happened with Hunt, that I weakened and took him to bed every night. But now, I didn't want to mention it. I should have stayed strong and said no. "No...he didn't give me any trouble. The presentation went well. Networked with Kyle Livingston. Saw a few other people there."

Thorn lifted his head and turned his expression on me. He narrowed his eyes and focused on me, reading my look like words on a page. He knew me better than anyone, and he picked up on the subtle changes in my tone and mood. "You aren't telling me something."

I held his gaze and considered my next move. I couldn't lie to him. We never did that to each other, and I didn't want to start now. He would judge me for what I did, reprimand me for being stupid, but I had to suffer the consequences. I made bad decisions. As my partner in life, it was his job to tell me the things I didn't want to hear. "One thing led to another...and I slept with Hunt."

Thorn leaned back into his chair, his broad shoulders straight and muscular. His expression didn't change, and his eyes didn't turn hostile. He continued to look at me with cloudy eyes, his thoughts unclear.

I waited for the judgment.

"Why?"

"It just happened. He kissed me, and I didn't stop it...you know how it goes."

"It just happened one time?"

"Uh...no."

His eyes narrowed.

"Every night we were there."

Thorn set down his fork and sighed. "Titan, what are you doing?"

"I wasn't thinking. I know he's accused of doing—"

"He's *guilty* of doing terrible things."

"I know. But I just...can't stop the way I feel about him. I know it's stupid and I know it's a mistake, but I can't help it. I fell so hard for him, and I can't keep my hands to myself. When he kisses me, I grow weak. When he tells me he loves me, I love hearing it. I know it's pathetic..."

Thorn sighed and looked down at the table. "I understand, Titan. It's not pathetic."

I couldn't stop the surprise from stretching across my face.

"But you need to be stronger than that. We have direct evidence that he's a liar. First, it was leaking the story to the newspapers. Then it was photographs of him and that woman in the club."

"But he released that story about him and his father so people would stop talking about it. And it worked."

"Maybe the reporter was never supposed to give up his name. And when he did, Hunt had to fix it."

"Maybe..."

Thorn eyed me, his sympathetic expression gone. "Titan, you need to be careful. You worked very hard to get here. It would be a shame to throw all that away for one man you can't trust."

His words sank into my heart and brought me back to reality. The pragmatic executive inside of me knew he was right. I was gambling more than I could afford to lose.

"I thought Hunt was the perfect match for you. But now, there's red flags all over the place. We can't ignore that. I always respect whatever decision you make. If you don't want to marry me, it's not a big deal. I'll be disappointed, but I'll get over it. So this isn't about me. It's about you. I know you don't need a man to protect you, but I want to protect you. You've been through enough as it is. I don't want to watch you repeat those terrible mistakes. I don't want you to start over for a third time."

I nodded in agreement. "You're right…"

"Every decision can easily be simplified. If he were a business deal, would you take it?"

There were too many unknown variables. I wouldn't put millions of dollars on the table for a deal this unpredictable. I'd turn my back and find something else to invest in. "No…"

"Then you have your answer."

I rested my elbows on the table and slowly dragged my hands down my face. My fingertips moved to my temples, and I gently massaged them even though I didn't have a migraine. My eyes took in the glow of the city, feeling Thorn stare at me with his protective gaze. I was grateful I had him in my life. This was exactly what I wanted, to have someone I could trust implicitly. How could I ever take a chance on Hunt when I had someone incredible sitting right beside me? We would never have passion or romance, but we would have something so much stronger. "I love you..." Thorn was my family, the only stability I ever truly had.

Thorn moved his hand across the table and rested his fingertips against my elbow. "I know."

"I want to believe him so much...sometimes I think I do." I never laid my feelings out on the table like this. Thorn was the only person I could open up to. Hunt was the second. He cracked me open like a clam and completely exposed me—and I allowed him to.

"I know."

"But you're right. I can't."

"Too risky."

"He told me he wanted to pick up our previous arrangement. I agreed."

Thorn pulled his hand away and stared at me until I met his gaze. "What if he tells everyone about the two of you?"

"He would have done it already."

"You think?"

"Why not tell the world about that in addition to the story he already leaked?"

Thorn didn't have an answer to that.

"Besides, he signed my NDA."

Thorn nodded.

"And whether I keep sleeping with him or not, he already has enough evidence to put me on blast. So it really doesn't make a difference."

"That's true. But sleeping with him could cloud your judgment."

"Not if it's just sex. And if I don't do this...I know it's going to happen anyway. At least this way, the relationship is controlled. There are rules. It keeps a physical relationship separate from an emotional one."

"I suppose. Once we're engaged, there's no going back. So that could protect you as well."

"Yeah..."

Thorn eyed me with his crystal blue eyes, which were soft and gentle. It was an expression he didn't show to anyone else but me. To the rest of the world, he was a cold and powerful businessman. He didn't have emotions. All he cared about was power, control, and money. But when it was just the two of us, he showed a different side. He was gentle, sweet, compassionate...and so much more. "Then you still want to marry me?"

I nodded.

"You need to give me a better answer than that."

"I do."

His cool eyes burned into my skin. He watched my

reaction, spotting my hesitation. "You're sure? Because you don't have to."

"No, I want to. It's the best decision."

"Is it?" he asked. "Because you could wait and fall in love with someone else."

Like that would ever happen. "No. Hunt is the last mistake I'll ever make. Romance doesn't work. It's painful and complicated. I want what we have. I want trust, friendship, stability...that's real love."

The intensity of his gaze lightened. "I agree. Just wanted to make sure you did too."

I nodded.

"Then I'll start preparing."

THE ELEVATOR slowly came to a stop then the doors opened.

I didn't tell Titan I was coming over. I didn't need to tell her a damn thing. I could have her when I wanted her—and she could have me whenever she pleased.

I stepped inside and saw her on the couch, folders and documents scattered on the table in front of her while her laptop remained on her thighs. Instead of a glass of whiskey, there was a glass of ice water on the sofa table.

Maybe she took my warning to heart.

Her green eyes were on me, and her lack of surprise suggested she'd anticipated my face before the doors even opened. She didn't rise to her feet or greet me with a hello. Sometimes she projected a cold exterior, but that was part of her business persona. I knew something was different now. Something was on her mind.

I'd worn a black blazer over my V-neck t-shirt, so I hung it up by the door. Her eyes immediately went to my shoulders, her favorite feature of mine. It was her favorite place to grip me whether she was on top or being plowed into the mattress.

I sat on the couch beside her and pulled the laptop off her lap. To protect her privacy, I closed it so she wouldn't wonder if I was looking at whatever she was working on. We used to have a solid foundation of trust, but now that was lost.

I missed it.

I missed the way she used to look at me—like I was the last person in the world who would ever hurt her. Now she stared at me with suspicion, second-guessing everything I said. No mask she wore was thick enough to hide the love in her eyes, but I wished there was more. I wished there was trust, friendship, and unflinching loyalty. "What is it?" I leaned back against the couch and turned my head toward her, smelling her perfume and hair shampoo mixed together. She was still in her pencil skirt and blouse, her heels sitting on the floor next to the other couch. Her hair was in loose curls, soft enough for me to run my fingers through.

She crossed her legs and straightened her posture, like this was a meeting between two partners, not two lovers.

"Don't do that."

She turned her cold expression on me. "Excuse me?"

"Don't put on a front. I want Tatum, not Titan."

"You don't get Tatum anymore. You'll never see her again. She's long gone."

The simple words drilled a hole right through my heart, hitting me in the sternum and fracturing the rest of my bones. Titan was a powerful woman with impressive looks and powerful intelligence. But Tatum was beautiful, compassionate, soft...and so much more. I wanted that woman—the woman I'd fallen in love with.

"You aren't to barge in here like that again. If you want to see me, you notify me first."

"Since when did we start this?"

"Now." She stared at me with a hard gaze.

"I don't reciprocate that. You can stop by my place whenever you damn well please, Titan. I have nothing to hide."

"Nor do I. But don't invade my space again."

When we last spoke, she was cold like this—but not so hard. Something had happened since I last saw her. Something influenced her to push me away like this. And I suspected I knew exactly who that was something was.

"I know this arrangement means something different to you than it does to me."

No.

"To me, it's just sex between two people. It's an exchange of fantasies. It's private and quiet. We don't talk about it with anyone else."

"I'm aware."

"But that's all it is. If you think it's going to lead to something more, I don't want to waste your time. I'm marrying Thorn. And I won't change my mind."

Like she'd smashed a sledgehammer against my heart, it cracked right down the middle. I knew she didn't love Thorn the way she loved me. I knew their relationship was nothing but a business arrangement. But that didn't stop me from being jealous—and terrified. I couldn't lose my woman over a crime I'd never committed. If I'd really wronged her, I'd be man enough to let her go. But that wasn't what happened, and I had to be man enough to fight for her. "Yes, you will."

"Hunt." Her voice became sterner, more powerful. "I won't change my mind."

"You don't love him."

"Exactly."

My jaw automatically tightened on its own, my teeth grinding together.

"If that's something you can't accept, then you should walk away. Despite what you did to me, I don't want to hurt you."

"I did nothing to you, Titan."

"Let's stop pretending you didn't sell my secrets to the world, and I'll stop pretending that I can keep my hands off you. I want this arrangement to continue because I don't want anyone else. I love our passion, our heat. You're the only man who can truly give me what I want. I could find someone else, but frankly, I don't want to. But I also want to marry Thorn, to spend the rest of my life with him and start a family. Those are my conditions. Take it or leave it."

She wasn't bluffing. I could feel it in the air around her. She must have told Thorn about our hookups in France, and he straightened her out. He made her hard as steel and cold as ice. I'd already made my case to her several times, and she didn't listen to me. I wasn't giving up, but I had to play by her rules. I would make her fall harder for me, rebuild the trust we lost, and I would change her mind before she handed herself over to Thorn. In the meantime, I would try to clear my name. They'd be engaged for a year. I had time. I wouldn't sleep with her when she was married because that would just make me sick to my stomach, knowing she was legally bound to someone else. Then I'd have to let her go—but only after I gave it all my effort. "There's a piece of the puzzle you're missing, a detail you overlooked."

Her eyes narrowed slightly. "And what is that?"

"Don't you think it's strange that the story came out after you told Thorn you wanted to marry me?"

Her expression didn't change, but I could tell her brain was working furiously to catch up to me, to understand my meaning before I revealed it to her.

"You said the three of us are the only people who know about that night. If I didn't tell anyone, then it must have been Thorn."

Her eyes narrowed. "Never."

"Well, I didn't do it. The guy may not be in love with you, but he's possessive of you. You think he'd let you go without a fight? He pretended to be supportive, but I bet he did this to get rid of me. It's the perfect crime. He risked potentially incriminating himself so he looks innocent."

"You're ridiculous."

"Am I?" I pressed. "It adds up to me."

Her eyes shifted slightly back and forth, her mind working at the speed of light.

"If you were mine, I'd do anything to keep you."

"Like accusing the one man I trust above everyone else?" she asked. "By making me question the only person who's ever had my back?"

I suspected Bruce Carol was the one behind this, but it could easily be Thorn. Bruce had no real way of getting access to that information. But Thorn knew every single detail because he'd lived through it. "It's a strange coincidence, Titan. Thorn has been planning on sharing his life with you for a long time. His parents adore you. You're already the richest woman in the world—not to mention the most gorgeous. He's ambitious and ruthless. He'd never find a woman more perfect than you. He knows that. So instead of letting you walk away, he sabotages the only competition—me."

Titan said nothing more, but her eyes kept shifting. She kept thinking, that brilliant brain of hers working at full speed. No matter how much she trusted Thorn, she had to admit that the timing was peculiar. Just before Thorn announced their mutual breakup to the world, that story hit the papers. Obviously, someone was framing me. Thorn was just as much of a suspect as Bruce Carol.

I kept staring into her eyes, hoping Titan would seriously consider my words and explore them. If she questioned Thorn about it, she might get some answers. She knew him better than anyone, so she could probably tell if he was lying. She was the best person to confront him. If I did it, I wouldn't get anywhere. "Ask him about it."

"He wouldn't do that to me." Her strength was gone, and only her quiet voice remained behind. She no longer seemed certain like she did just moments ago.

"It doesn't hurt to ask."

"You're turning me against him."

I shook my head slightly. "I'm trying to get to the truth. I wasn't the one who sold you out, and that means someone else is out to get you. I have to find out who that person is, not just for my sake—but for yours. I have to protect you. Whether you want me to or not, I have to make sure you're okay. I'm not gonna let someone ruin everything you worked so hard for. You're the most incredible person I've ever met. Even if you turn your back on me, I'm never going to turn my back on you."

Her mask broke, and Tatum started to shine through. She was impervious to criticism and cruelty, but when I put my heart on the line, she was vulnerable to it. Her soul opened just to take it in. "Diesel... I've never been so confused in my life. I want to believe you...more than anything."

I cupped her face and kissed her, giving her a gentle embrace. My heart melted into hers as we connected. I breathed with her, and she breathed back. There was nothing that made me feel more at peace than when I kissed her, when I shared everything I had with my woman. When I was with Tatum, my life felt complete. She felt the same way. I could feel it in the shake of her fingertips, the way her breathing changed simply because I touched her. "Just ask him. Please."

"I don't know. If he didn't do it, it's very insulting."

"You have to ask, Titan. I understand that you can't take my word for it, not when it's too risky. But if you love me, at least ask. Just give me the benefit of the doubt and ask."

She rested her forehead against mine and closed her eyes.

"Baby."

"I'll do it."

I squeezed her hand. "Thank you."

"If he says no...then I don't want to talk about it anymore. I want this just to be an arrangement, only sex and nothing else. I'm giving you a chance to clear your name. If you don't, then I have to move forward."

I knew that would be her attitude. "I'll figure it out. One way or another."

"I hope you do."

---

I'D BEEN MANAGING MY EVER-GROWING EMPIRE FOR OVER ten years, and not once did I feel overwhelmed by stress. I did what I needed to do and focused on the job. Shit always got in the way, but I found ways of overcoming those obstacles.

But I was terrified I would lose Titan.

She was slowly slipping away from me, being influenced by a man she trusted above everyone else. She told me that she was going to marry him, that she had committed to it. Unless a miracle happened and I managed to put everything to rest, she wouldn't be mine anymore.

I couldn't let that happen.

Titan was the first woman to make me feel something. She made me feel passion, lust, excitement. She got me rock-hard and violently aroused. And she made me feel softer emotions, like compassion, loyalty, love, and everything in between. She brought me back to life when I'd only felt numb. She made me feel joy for the first time in my adult life. She was more valuable than my net worth. All the money in the world couldn't make me feel as good as she did.

I wanted her for the rest of my life.

I'd die if Thorn got to keep her, if he got to have her without even falling in love with her. It was a total waste. Titan deserved more. She deserved to be loved by a man who gave her his entire heart, who put everything on the line to love her so deeply.

Someone like me.

I wasn't a romantic guy, but I sure as hell loved that woman with everything I had.

I sat at my desk and kept thinking everything over, wondering if she'd spoken to Thorn about my accusation. I didn't want to believe he would do that to her, sabotage her happiness in such a vile way. I'd rather have him be the upstanding man she believed he was instead of the rat I feared he could be. But at least I could get my answer and move on.

Natalie spoke through the intercom. "Mr. Hunt?" Her lack of confidence was apparent the second she said my name. "Mr. Hunt is here to see you."

All thoughts of Titan disappeared. My eyes shifted to the small speaker on my desk, and I felt my heart immediately increase in pace. Jax had called me once to warn me about our father. I never expected him to stop by. Whatever he had to say must have been important if he came all the way down here. No doubt it had to do with the story I spilled to the entire world. "Send Jax in, Natalie."

"Uh...it's not Jax Hunt."

Now my heart stopped altogether.

"It's Vincent Hunt."

My office had never been so quiet. I had never felt so alone but so suffocated at the very same instant. I hadn't seen my father in years, hardly gave him any thought. Now he was standing right outside my doors, probably fuming with hostility. I wasn't afraid of my father, but I didn't exactly feel comfortable with him showing up on my territory. This was my world that he'd stepped into.

But I knew exactly what this was about. He'd been pissed I took Megaland, but now he was livid that I'd tarnished his reputation to everyone in the world. I could never give him the real reason why I did it, so I'd have a hard time explaining my actions.

Natalie spoke again. "Should I send him in?"

The cowardly thing to do would be to refuse him. And I definitely wasn't a coward. "Yes."

"I'll send him right in."

I only had a minute to prepare for his entrance,

but there was no mental preparation I could undertake to anticipate the conversation. Perhaps he was just there to yell at me, but that wasn't his style. The only terminology he used was veiled threats. That was the only way he communicated with people.

The door opened, and he stepped inside.

He was my height, six foot three, with broad shoulders and a trim physique. He was in his fifties, but he looked like a man who'd just hit forty. He still had the musculature of a strong man in his youth, arms tight with muscle and a slim waistline. He wore a gray suit with a matching tie. His dress shoes were shiny, probably because he never wore the same pair for longer than a week. One hand rested in his pocket, while the other swung by his side. His deep brown eyes were on me.

He didn't blink.

I didn't blink.

It was quiet.

So fucking quiet.

His shoes tapped against the hardwood floor, but the sound was drowned by our mutual hostility.

He approached my desk, unfastened his button, and dropped into the chair.

Now we were face-to-face, eye level, and mutually aggressive. He waged a war against me with that cold stare. His chin was covered with thick stubble, the kind I got when I didn't shave for over a week. His brown eyes seemed darker than mine, resembling black tar more than tree bark. He wore a flashy watch along with his expensive suit. He didn't wear a wedding ring because he never remarried after my mother was gone. My father and I had a startling resemblance. People mistook us for brothers sometimes. He'd aged well, and I felt like I was looking into a time machine. I just hoped I wouldn't be so bitter, angry, and spiteful when I reached my fifties. Jax looked similar to him, but not the way I did. I was his firstborn son, and that was probably why he was so much harsher with me than he was with Jax.

More tense silence.

More absent threats.

More stares.

I held his gaze and hardly blinked, remaining rigid in the silent standoff. He thought he had the upper hand because he showed up on my doorstep, but I was the one dealing with his visit without any warning. That gave me the upper hand—a million times over.

I could start by explaining my actions when I shared personal information with the press, but since I didn't have a real explanation, I chose to remain silent. I didn't want to mention Titan in any context. I didn't want him to hear her name, to know she even existed. So I kept my silence.

"You shouldn't have fucked with me, Diesel." Deep and powerful, he spoke with the authority he'd had since I could remember. He'd always been a wealthy businessman. He'd owned most of the world since I was a child. He was used to pushing people around until he got what he wanted. He was an elitist, assuming he was better than others simply because he was a self-made man. His DNA was more important than anyone else's. Brett would never be human since he wasn't his son. "I've let you crawl around like a cockroach in the house because you weren't worth my time to squish. But not anymore. You know what I do to my enemies. You know what's coming."

I wasn't intimidated by this man. If I were, I wouldn't have turned my back on him in the first place. My father and I had had a good relationship. When he cast Brett out, I didn't want to declare war against him. But to do nothing made me just as guilty, so I had to take a stand. I had to do the right thing. I had to be there for my brother. "If my mother were still alive, she'd be ashamed of you." She had a beautiful spirit that counteracted my father's coldness. She never cared about money. She still cooked all our meals because she enjoyed it. She still took us to the park on a sunny day so we could toss a football around. She never wanted a fancy car or expensive jewels. All she wanted was for us to be a family.

His expression didn't change, my words bouncing off his exterior like they had no impact at all. "And I'm ashamed of you, Diesel. We've had our differences, but I've never been so humiliated to call you my son."

I had the exact same reaction, pretending his words didn't infect me like a poison. Like what he said didn't matter, my features were etched in stone and didn't change. But those words sank into my frame and damaged my heart. I was paralyzed by what he'd said. I knew he despised me, but hearing him actually say it was crippling. I wasn't an emotional man. Never had been. But those words hurt—badly. "I didn't go to the press to hurt you."

"I know exactly why you did it."

That wasn't possible, so I waited for an explanation. I couldn't ask more of him because that would only make him reveal less.

"You picked Tatum Titan over your own family. Unforgivable."

I struggled to keep up my neutral expression even more. Pretending to be indifferent was nearly impossible once her name was mentioned. My father's assumption was right on the money. It was exactly why I did what I did. But how did he know? I couldn't ask, so I didn't.

He rose to his feet and adjusted his cuff links without taking his gaze off me. "You shouldn't have fucked with me, Diesel. Now it's my turn to fuck with you."

## 10

TITAN

I DREADED CONFRONTING Thorn about Hunt's suspicion. It was a huge insult if I was wrong. After everything we'd been through, it was painful to accuse him of something that seemed so impossible. He'd been everything to me for the past decade. There was no one in the world I trusted more than him.

As much as I wanted Hunt to be cleared, I didn't want him to be right about this.

I couldn't lose Thorn.

I stopped by his penthouse after work. He was home, having just showered after his session with his personal trainer. He was in gray sweatpants and a t-shirt. His hair was slightly damp because he usually dried his hair with a towel.

"What's up?" he asked as he greeted me in front of the elevator. "Your turn to raid my fridge?"

"Like there's anything in there. You're practically a garbage disposal."

He chuckled as he headed to the kitchen. "A man like me needs fuel. I don't look like this from starving myself." He opened the cabinets and made a drink for me and grabbed a beer for himself. He carried it to the living room then turned on the TV. "The game is coming on in an hour. You wanna hang around and watch it?"

"No company tonight?"

"Nah." He drank his beer then set it on the coaster. "I had this woman over for the weekend. Still trying to recuperate, if you know what I mean." He nudged me in the side and winked.

"It's pretty clear," I said sarcastically. "You like her?"

"Yeah, she's gorgeous. Doesn't speak much English though."

"Where did you meet her?"

"I had a business meeting, and the guy brought his Russian wife along."

I raised an eyebrow. "You slept with the guy's wife?"

"No," he said with a laugh. "She brought her sister along. I hooked up with her. Then she went back to Russia on Monday."

"Now it all makes sense."

"Russian women…" He whistled under his breath. "My god, they're beautiful." He rested one arm over the back of the couch and looked at the TV. "What's new with you? How'd your day go?"

"It was good. I had a meeting that went longer than it should have, and it messed up my entire day."

"Hate it when that happens. My assistant brings a timer. When that goes off, I'm outta there no matter what."

It wasn't so simple for me. Men constantly talked over me and tried to take control of the meeting —unsuccessfully.

Thorn took another drink of his beer then returned it to the coaster. "Something wrong with your drink?"

"No." I hadn't cared about it because I was focusing all my attention on this dreadful conversation. The longer I sat there with him, the more unlikely Hunt's theory seemed. Could Thorn really do that to me and then listen to me confess how much I loved Hunt? How would he be able to sleep at night knowing he was causing me so much pain?

"Well, you haven't even taken a drink." He turned his gaze toward me, his eyes narrowed with accusation.

"I'm trying to cut back."

His eyebrow cocked. "Please don't tell me you're pregnant."

I rolled my eyes. "Of course not. I really am just trying to cut back."

"Why?"

"I drink too much."

"Says who?" he questioned. "We all drink. Who cares?"

"I'm not quitting, just trying to taper it down a little."

Thorn finally stopped the interrogation and turned back to the TV.

I didn't even know how to broach the subject. I didn't know where to begin or how to start. If I came right out and asked the question, it could be too harsh and unpredictable.

"Is there something wrong, Titan?" he asked without looking at me. "I'm getting some weird vibes from you. You aren't yourself right now."

"I have something on my mind..."

Thorn ignored the TV and looked at me, granting me an attentive look. He gave me his complete focus, turning into the friend that I'd known for the ten years. He cared about everything I had to say. It was hard to believe this man could ever do something so deceitful. I was about to ask him about it, and I still couldn't believe it could possibly be true. "I was talking to Hunt yesterday..."

"That can't be good."

"And he said something to me that I haven't been able to get out of my head. I wanted to talk to you about it."

"I'm listening." He gave me the same stare, waiting for me to continue.

Something in my gut told me this wouldn't go over well, but I had to ask. "Hunt mentioned it was a strange coincidence that the news story came out directly after I told you I wanted to be with him."

His expression didn't change.

"He insists he isn't the one who went to the newspapers. And since only the three of us knew about it, he thinks you are a possible suspect. You didn't want to let me go, so you got rid of Hunt by framing him."

Instead of getting angry, he let a slow smile creep onto his face. "Wow. That guy is desperate, isn't he?"

His reaction wasn't setting off any alarm bells, but he didn't state he thought Hunt's assumption was wrong. "Is he...?"

Thorn's smile faded away once he read the room. This wasn't some ridiculous accusation that I'd brushed off. It wasn't impossible, even though it was extremely unlikely. When he saw the seriousness in my eyes, his mouth tightened in a deep frown. "Wait, you're actually buying into this?"

"Not at all. But I wanted to talk to you about it."

"Talk to me about what, exactly?" His hostility grew like a fire that just been fed a splash of gasoline.

"Are you denying the accusation?"

He threw his arms down and rolled his eyes. "You're kidding me, right? Do I really need to answer that question?"

I stared him down.

His eyes filled with pain when he realized I was being serious. "No, Titan. I didn't sell your story to the newspapers just to get rid of the man you love. I didn't risk life in jail just to keep him away from you. For the past ten years, I've only been your rock and you've been mine. The world has turned against us countless times, but we've always stood shoulder to shoulder. To think I would betray you in such a manipulative and cunning way...is disgusting. The fact that you doubted me, even for a second, is... There are no words." He rose from the couch and ran his hands through his hair.

"I didn't mean to offend you—"

"Well, you did."

I rose to my feet and faced him, watching the flustered look on his face. "Hunt pressured me to ask you. He insists he didn't do this, and he wants to figure out who did. His suspects are you and Bruce Carol."

Thorn's normally fair skin had a tint of red. His blue eyes were cold like ice, and his chest rose and fell dramatically with the deep breaths he took. He was angry, his rage slowly building and filling the entire room. "And he's the biggest suspect of all, Titan. Why do you keep forgetting that?"

"I haven't forgotten."

"Seems like you have. This asshole is the one who betrayed you, and now he's turning you against me. In case you've forgotten, I was the one who stabbed Jeremy in the heart to protect you." He slammed his fist against his chest. "I was the one who gave you your first loan. I'm the one who's always got your back and your front. One pretty man walks into your life, and you forget all of that? You strip away everything that's so damn good about our relationship just because he plants a ridiculous idea in your head? I thought you were smarter than that, Titan. But it looks like you never learn after all."

My tongue suddenly felt too big for my mouth, and I felt too weak to stand.

"Get out." He turned away from me, shaking his head like he'd never been so disappointed in me.

"Thorn, I never accused you. I just wanted—"

"Yes, you did. The fact that you even had to ask is a demonstration of how much you've lost your mind. Get out of my house and don't come back."

My heart slipped all the way down to my stomach. "Thorn—"

"Don't make me ask a third time, Titan." He walked out of the living room and into the hallway. I knew he was in his bedroom when I heard the door shut behind him. The TV was still on, his beer was covered in condensation. A commercial came on the screen, and it was about insurance.

I didn't go after him because he needed his space. He'd never walked away from me like that before. He'd never asked me to leave. He'd never turned his back on me the way he did now.

I let myself out.

———

I SAT IN THE DARK FOR HOURS, THINKING ABOUT MY conversation with Thorn. I felt like shit. I felt worse than I did when that article about me was published. I felt like I'd lost a piece of myself, lost a family member.

It was like losing my father all over again.

My instinct was to call Thorn and apologize. But he wouldn't take my calls. He was angry with me, and what he needed right now was space. Pestering him wouldn't get me anywhere. I would give it a week before I tried to speak to him again.

I felt like an idiot for asking him that stupid question.

I dragged my hand across my face and sighed, feeling the distant ache in my entire chest. It was the painful precursor to tears, the beginning of an action I worked so hard to avoid. I didn't let a single tear fall, but keeping it in was somehow more painful.

My phone rang.

I grabbed it and hoped to see Thorn's name on the screen.

But it was Hunt.

I didn't feel like talking right now, so I silenced his call and set it on the cushion beside me.

He didn't leave a voice mail, but a text message popped up. *I need to talk to you.*

I could feel the urgency in his message. It was the only thing that caught my attention in that moment. I was in pain, but for some reason, his pain seemed more important to me. I picked up the phone and called him.

His deep voice filled the silence. "Hey." He seemed

down, like he'd already heard the news about Thorn and me. He only said a single word, but the pain in his tone was heavy. It was unmistakable.

"Hey…" I couldn't speak without my voice cracking. I was a master at hiding my emotions from everyone, but with Hunt, all my skills were useless. He could crack through my hard shell with a single word.

His concern exploded through the phone. "Baby, what's wrong?"

I shouldn't let him call me that anymore, but it felt so nice. It blanketed me with his affection, his love. It was like being cradled in his big, strong arms without his even being there. "I talked to Thorn…"

He sighed into the phone. "What happened?"

I didn't have the energy to tell the entire story. Reliving it would just be painful. "Denied the claim… and then was hurt that I would ever suspect him doing something like that. Told me to get out of his penthouse and…not to come back." I struggled to keep my voice steady, but it was useless. It kept shaking. The pain and emotion combined together to make a single storm.

He sighed again. "I'll be right there, alright?"

I shouldn't want to see him, but that was the only thing I wanted. Nothing sounded better than having his masculine kisses all over my body, his comforting words spoken directly into my ear while his powerful arms protected me from the coldness of my reality. "Okay."

He arrived less than ten minutes later and helped himself inside my penthouse. The elevator doors opened, and he headed right toward me. His heavy body sank into the couch and his arm wrapped around me, pulling me against his chest, right where I wanted to be. His lips brushed against my hairline, giving me a kiss that was more searing than the kind he gave when he was between my legs. His breath fell across my neck, and he felt perfectly comfortable positioned that way.

I wrapped my arm around his waist and snuggled into his side. I didn't talk about Thorn because there was nothing more to be said. I'd hurt his feelings, and I wished I could take it back.

"I'm sorry."

"It's not your fault."

"It is my fault," he whispered. "I told you to ask him."

"And I shouldn't have listened to you…"

His body stiffened in reaction. "He seemed sincere when he said it wasn't him?"

I nodded. "And if he was just doing it to get rid of

you, he ended up getting rid of me himself. So your theory is debunked."

"He didn't get rid of you. He'll come around."

"You didn't see him."

His lips brushed over my temple, and he placed a kiss on my forehead. "I had to know it wasn't him."

"And he still thinks it's you."

"It's not me," he whispered. "I promise it isn't me."

"And you told me to accuse Thorn because you knew this would happen...that I would push him away."

"What do I get out of that?" he asked. "Seeing the woman I love almost in tears? I have kinky tastes, but I'm not into that."

I moved away from his touch and sat upright on the couch. I looked at the floor, avoiding his gaze. "I wish I could undo all of this. He seemed so hurt by what I said. I feel terrible."

"I promise you, he'll come around."

"Even if he does, it won't be the same. I violated our trust."

"All you did was ask a question. You didn't accuse him of it."

"It's the same thing—we both know it."

His hand moved into my hair, and he forced my gaze on him. His brown eyes were warm like hot coffee, and his t-shirt fit snugly against his frame. He looked sad in a way I'd never seen him before. He hurt when I hurt, but this was different. It seemed like he was troubled on a deeper level. "Is there something wrong?"

He held my gaze, his fingers moving through my soft hair until they reached the tips. His eyes glanced down, and he looked at my hair as it stretched across my shoulders. His hand traveled between my shoulder blades and down my back. His pregnant pause stretched on with no end in sight. "No."

"When we spoke on the phone, you seemed down."

"Just missed you." His eyes moved up again, his brown eyes no longer easy to read like a book. He seemed to be hiding something, a thought or an emotion. "I'm sorry you're in pain, baby. I hate seeing you like this. I know how much he means to you. He's more than a friend...he's family."

"Yes...he is."

"He'll come around."

I bowed my head because I didn't believe him. There was a finality to our conversation, like things would never be the same between Thorn and me. He was the best thing that ever happened to me, the best friend any person could ask for. Now he was gone.

"Try talking to him again."

"I need to give him space. He's too angry right now."

Hunt grabbed my hand and leaned toward me. He pressed a kiss to my shoulder and rested his mouth there. "Tell me what I can do."

I didn't want to think about it anymore. I wanted a distraction, something to take my mind off the throbbing pain inside my heart. I wanted a clear head so I could get some sleep. Otherwise, I wouldn't get any rest for the next week. "Fuck me. Fuck me until I can't keep my eyes open anymore."

# 11

HUNT

I'D CALLED Titan to tell her about my father.

About the insulting conversation that took place in my office.

He threatened me. Said he despised me. Wanted to make my life miserable.

As a man, it took a lot to wound me. I was covered in layers of muscle, but also built with steel. My skin was tough like hide, and it was difficult to land a blow that actually affected me. But my father's words cut me all the way to the bone. I was still bleeding even though the wounds were invisible.

I made my peace with the fact that I didn't have a relationship with my father. I had my reasons, and my reasons were good enough. But I'd never hated him, and it hurt to know that he hated me.

My mother would be disappointed in both of us, not just him.

We stood on opposite sides of the battlefield, and neither one of us was willing to call a truce. I set off an explosion that I couldn't take back in order to win Titan back. She still couldn't trust me, and I wasn't sure if it'd all been for nothing.

I hoped not.

But when I arrived at her penthouse, she was on the verge of tears. Titan was just as strong as I was, and she hid her emotions deep below the surface. She wasn't the kind of person who cried when something tore her down. She spent her energy finding a solution to her problem, not moping about it. Seeing the wetness in her eyes told me how much she ached. The sadness written all over her face made me feel so depressed. I couldn't mention my own pain when she was the only thing that really mattered. I was hoping to drop my armor and let her tend to my wounds. Instead, I hid them away and pretended I wasn't bleeding at all.

This was all my fault.

I thought there was a good chance that Thorn was the one who betrayed her, but since Titan didn't have a doubt he was telling the truth, I had to rule him out as a suspect. That left me with only one culprit, and I had to pursue it until I got some answers.

But for now, I had to make this right.

Which was why I was walking up to Thorn's assistant inside his building. "I need to see Mr. Cutler."

"Do you have an appointment?" She looked up at me from under her thick eyelashes, taking in my features without being discreet about it.

Titan would be jealous. "No. But it's important."

"Your name?"

This part would be tricky. "Diesel Hunt."

"I'll see if he's available." She picked up the phone and spoke with him directly. "There's a Diesel Hunt here to speak with you. He says it's urgent." When she heard his response, her features hardened slightly. "Okay, sir." She hung up and hardly looked at me. "He says he's too busy to help a little bitch like you...his words, not mine."

My temper would normally rise to an insult like this, but right now, it didn't matter. I turned away from her desk and walked right into Thorn's office.

"Sir, wait!"

I shut the door and drowned out her voice. I entered his office and saw him sitting behind his enormous desk, his eyes on me. They were cold and hostile, full of unfettered rage. "Get the fuck out, Hunt."

"Just listen to me." I held up a hand as I slowly approached his desk. I stood farther back than I normally would, not wanting to make this more confrontational than it already was.

"I don't have to do a damn thing. Now get out before I call security."

They'd better have guns because that was the only thing that would stop me. "Don't be upset with Titan. I was the one who told her my suspicions. I know you don't believe I'm innocent, but I am. I have to find out who's behind this because Titan has an enemy. I don't want something worse to happen to her."

Thorn gave me a blank look like none of that meant anything to him. "Titan might believe your bullshit, but I don't. The only reason why my sleeves aren't rolled up and my knuckles aren't against your face is because I'm in my office. Now if we were in a dark alley somewhere, I'd be putting your dead body in a dumpster right now."

His anger matched Titan's when she'd first read the article. She slapped me several times, hit me hard enough that my cheek was red for nearly a day. "I saw Titan last night. Her eyes were full of tears, and she was devastated. She's scared that she's lost the most important person in her life. When I first accused you, she rejected the idea and said it was impossible. It took nearly thirty minutes just for her to agree to run it by you."

His anger dimmed, but not substantially. "You're trying to rip us apart. How does she not see that?"

"Then why am I standing here trying to put you back together?"

Thorn clenched his jaw, the hard lines of his face deepening.

"Forgive her. Please."

He rested his fingertips against his lip, his eyes still ice-cold. "What do you want, Hunt? What are you after?"

"What's that supposed to mean?"

"You betray her, and then you spend all this time trying to convince her otherwise. What's the point of it all? Why don't you just admit you fucked her over and move on? Did you plan to do it but then fell for her? And now you're trying to make up for it?"

"No. I didn't do it, Thorn. Someone framed me."

"Why?" he demanded. "Even if that's true, what's the motive?"

"I don't know. But what's the motive for me to betray her? There is none."

"Just because I don't see the motive doesn't mean

there isn't one," he said coldly. "You've been messing with her for too long, Hunt. If you have any respect for the woman, just leave her alone. She's already agreed to marry me, so that's off the table. There's nothing left for you."

"She's not marrying you."

"Really?" He tilted his head to the side. "Because when we spoke last night before she accused me, she said that's what she wanted."

"For now. But I'll change her mind."

Thorn shook his head.

"Does that mean you forgive her?"

All I got was a stare.

"If you still plan to marry her...?"

He lowered his fingers from his mouth and rested his hand on the arm of his chair. "I'm still pretty pissed at her. But I'm sure we'll work it out...eventually."

"If I tell her to come by your place tonight, will you see her?"

He turned his head away and looked at the book-shelf on the other wall. "Yeah, I guess. If she's that upset about it, I don't want her to keep feeling that way. I was just angry, and I let my temper get carried away..."

"She thinks you never want to see her again."

"She tends to assume the worst possible conclusion."

I didn't step closer to his desk, keeping my distance behind one of his armchairs. "I know I said this already, but I didn't do it."

Thorn didn't give me a look of sympathy.

"I need you to believe me."

"What's the motive for someone to frame you?" he asked.

I repeated his words back to him. "Just because you don't see a motive doesn't mean it's not there."

Thorn sighed and rose from his chair. "All I have is your word, Hunt. Everything else stacks up against you, especially that blonde you were kissing."

"I gave her a ride home. That's it."

"That's not what the photograph showed."

"Why would I go home with her when I can have Titan every night?" I demanded. "That's the only field I'm sowing my seeds in. Why would I settle for some ordinary woman when I can have the sexiest woman on the planet? Doesn't add up."

"It doesn't add up to me either. But neither does that photo."

I would never dig myself out of this hole, not when both of them didn't believe me. The odds over-whelmed me. Not only did I have to convince Titan I was innocent, but also her closest friend. Now my father wanted to destroy me, and I had to clear my name before I ran out of time. In addition to that, I had to keep running my businesses. It's not like I could ever take time off from my work. I wanted to scream in frustration, but that wouldn't get me anywhere.

"I see what Titan means." He stood behind his desk with both of his hands in his pockets.

I cocked my head to the side, waiting for an elaboration.

"She wants to believe you. There's something about you that makes her question the evidence staring her right in the face. And I see it too…see something that makes me wonder if you're telling the truth."

Hope was just served to me on a platter. It wasn't much, but it was something. "I am."

"Then give us something to prove it."

"It's not so simple."

"And it's not so simple for us to believe you, Hunt."

———

I PULLED INTO BRETT'S DRIVEWAY IN CONNECTICUT then walked up to the front door. I rang the doorbell and heard the loud sound through the solid wood door.

"It's open."

I walked inside and moved into his living room where he had the game on the enormous TV on the wall. He had two beers on the coffee table, and he popped off the lid of one before he handed it to me. "Here."

"Thanks." I took it then set it down again, not interested in drinking. I took a seat. "We need to talk."

"What's up?" He drank his beer as he kept his eyes on the game.

I waited for him to look at me, and when he didn't, I grabbed the remote and turned off the screen.

"What the hell?"

"This is important."

"It better be pretty damn important because this is the finals."

It was definitely more important than that. "My father stopped by my office yesterday."

Brett's jaw slowly dropped, and his eyes widened in shock. "Vincent Hunt stopped by your office?"

"Yeah."

"Oh shit." He set the beer down hard and spilled some of it across the surface. Drops got on his hand, but he didn't seem to notice the cold liquid. "What happened?"

"He was pissed about the article."

"No surprise there. Anyone would be pissed."

"Somehow, he knew exactly why I did it. He knew it was because of Titan."

"How?"

I shrugged. "I have absolutely no idea. Baffles me. Maybe he's been keeping tabs on me since Megaland."

"Do you think he's the one who actually told the reporter about Titan?"

I hadn't considered that. "I don't know. I can't think of any reason why he would know about that."

"Well, someone outside the three of you knew about it. So that information was accessible."

"True…and Jax did warn me he was pissed."

"Maybe it was him," Brett said. "I wouldn't put it past him. He's a psychopath."

"I guess it's possible. If he knew about my relationship with Titan, he might have wanted to sabotage it. But that doesn't sound like his style. He doesn't care about my personal relationships. All he cares about is business."

"That's true," Brett said in agreement. "But he does know you're sleeping with Titan."

"Maybe he figured it out once that article came

out. When I tried to bury her story with my own story, that could have been a red flag to him. He is observant."

"Yeah, that's true."

My life was so simple before Titan walked into it. Now it was more complicated than it'd ever been.

"What do you think he's going to do?"

"Hopefully, nothing against Titan."

"She's not involved in your feud, so I think she's safe. She is a powerful business guru in his world. Doesn't make sense for him to make enemies with her when he's already got to deal with you."

That comforted me—just a little.

"I say he's only going to go after you."

It was a testament to my love for her that I was actually relieved by that notion. All I wanted was to be with Titan, even if everything was stripped away from me. My father could do his worst to destroy my empire, but it didn't matter. None of that meant as much as it did before.

"Have you told her?"

"No."

"Why?" he asked.

When I planned to open my heart to her, she was already heartbroken. The last thing she needed was to worry about my problems when she had her own. "I haven't had a chance. A lot of other things are going on right now."

"What's your next plan?"

I shook my head. "Not a clue. Everything is so fucked up right now." I dragged my hand across my temple and into my hair.

"Where do the two of you stand?"

"We're together...but barely."

"That's good. Covering up her story must have meant something to her."

"Yeah...but she doesn't trust me. We're kinda just hooking up right now. Everything is different. It's like she's walking on eggshells all the time."

"She'll come around."

"I don't know..."

"If she's still with you after everything that's happened, then that's a good sign. She loves you, and there's no way she doesn't know that you love her too." He wiped his arm with a napkin then took a drink of his beer.

"I hope you're right."

"The dust has to settle eventually. You just have to find out who pulled the trigger, and everything will go back to what it was."

"If only it were that easy..."

"You suspect Bruce Carol?"

I nodded. "I can't think of anyone else. Thought it could be Thorn, but that was a dead end."

"Then question him."

"I'm trying to figure out how. Maybe I'll just have my guy tail him."

"But the damage has been done. I think interrogation is the only thing that will work."

I nodded in agreement.

"And maybe you should take Titan with you. Because if you get anything out of him, she's going to want that evidence for herself."

Could I get Titan to come along with me? I'd already convinced her to accuse Thorn, and that blew up in her face. The odds of getting her to interrogate a man she hated seemed unlikely. "I'll see what I can do."

## 12

TITAN

THE SECOND I GOT HOME, I made a drink.

I wasn't cutting back anymore.

Feeling that burn down my throat, the tingle in my fingertips, the fog in the back of my eyes...kept me sane. All day, I wore my authoritative mask with a feminine smile. I got work done without anyone questioning my wellness. No one had a clue that I was barely keeping my head above water.

I wanted to call Thorn so many times.

He needed space, so I refrained from smothering him with my apologies. I knew him better than anyone, and he needed time to cool off before he could have a reasonable conversation. Since I'd accused him of something so awful, he would need at least a week to come back down to earth.

Being patient had never been so difficult.

I slipped off my heels in my living room and pulled my knees to my chest. A cherry floated on the surface of my drink, and an orange peel was wedged onto the glass. I stared at the ice cubes as they slowly melted and shifted.

The light above the elevator brightened, and a quiet sound beeped into my penthouse. Someone was just about to step into my home. Only two people had access to my elevator. Thorn was one of the two, but he definitely wasn't coming by for a visit.

Which meant it was Hunt.

The doors opened, and Thorn walked inside, still dressed in his suit and tie. His hair was styled, his eyes were bright, and he stepped into my penthouse with his hands in his pockets.

I stared at him blankly, unsure if I was really looking at him. After our difficult conversation yesterday, I didn't expect to see him for a while. And I definitely didn't expect him to come to me.

I returned my feet to the floor and straightened in the chair. I watched him walk toward me, hostility absent from his expression. I was usually good with words, but now I couldn't think of a single coherent sentence to utter. The surprise hadn't washed away just yet.

He sat in the armchair facing the couch and

crossed his ankle on the opposite knee. His black suit fit him perfectly, and he looked completely at home in my penthouse. His eyes scanned the room for a moment, as if looking to see if someone else was there. Then his eyes settled on me, without anger.

Now that he was planted in the armchair with no intention of leaving, I finally found my voice. "It's really nice to see you."

His hands came together in front of him while his elbows rested on the armrests.

"I was just sitting here thinking about you."

"I've been thinking about you a lot too."

I swallowed since my throat was dry. Thorn was the only person in the world who made me feel truly at ease. I didn't need to erect a single wall because there was no need for protection. Knowing that I might have lost something so rare was utterly terrifying. "I already apologized, but I'll say it again. I'm sorry, Thorn. I never should have even entertained the idea that you would do something like that..."

He slightly raised his hand, silencing me. "It's okay, Titan. I forgive you."

He did? He kicked me out of his penthouse yesterday. He turned his back on me and gave me the cold shoulder. What happened between yesterday and today? "Really?"

"Really."

"I feel like I'm missing something." I searched Thorn's gaze for an answer, needing an explanation for the sudden shift.

He rubbed the knuckles of his left hand. "Hunt stopped by my office today."

As with any other time his name was mentioned, I went rigid. No other man made me feel so weak and so strong at the same time. He had a potent effect on me. My heart was wrapped around his finger and tied by an unbreakable knot. "Oh?"

"Said he was the one with the suspicion. That he pressured you to mention it to me."

Once again, Hunt did something extremely sweet for me. All of his actions directly contradicted the crimes he was accused of. He didn't have to go to Thorn at all, but he suffered a difficult conversation just to make me happy.

"He also said how much you were hurting." He looked into my gaze with his piercing eyes. "Said you were on the verge of tears."

I didn't let the emotion creep into my face now. I was embarrassed I'd shed so many tears in the past month. It wasn't like me at all. "You know how much I love you, Thorn. You're all I have in this cruel world. We have something special. I'd be devastated if I lost it. You're my brother, my father, my everything. You're the only stable thing I have in my life. You're my rock. I don't want to picture my life without you in it."

Thorn continued to watch me with his icy gaze, his palms slowly sliding past one another. His anger was gone, but there was something else that had replaced it. "I was hurt by the accusation because it's so ridiculous."

"I know…"

"It confuses me that so much has changed since Hunt came into the picture. It used to be the two of us against the world. And now everything is so complicated. I miss our old simplicity."

"I know what you mean."

"I want it to be the way it was," he said quietly. "I want it to be the two of us first—Hunt second. There's so much distrust surrounding him, and neither one of us knows what to make of it. We can't let it affect our lives like this. He could be trying to rip us apart on purpose, and we nearly allowed him to do it."

"I don't think he's trying to rip us apart."

"I don't think so either. But he could be. The fact that I'm not sure worries me. Nothing about him is concrete. And the weirdest part is…a part of me wants to believe him."

I wanted to believe him too.

"But this isn't us. We don't take risks. We don't make bets unless we already know the outcome. We're changing our lives because of this one guy. Unless he has something specific to provide us, we can't keep moving backward."

"I know."

"So we need to decide what we're going to do—together."

I crossed my legs, feeling like we were in a meeting. "What do you mean?"

"About Hunt. Do you think there's any truth to what he's saying?"

"I...I don't know. Sometimes I think he could be telling the truth. Sometimes I believe him. But since I'm in love with him...my judgment isn't the best."

Thorn rested his fingertips against his temple. "There are too many unknowns. I think there's a slight possibility he could be telling the truth, but I wouldn't gamble on it. We can't change our lives for such a slim possibility."

"Change our lives how?" I asked.

"By not turning on each other. By getting married. We need to move forward with our plans and not let him affect our lives anymore."

My gaze shifted to my hands.

"We need to give him a timetable to clear his

name. If he doesn't do it in that time frame, we need to move on with our lives. We're falling behind. We were supposed to be engaged a month ago."

"How much time should we give him?"

Thorn paused as he considered it. "Two weeks."

Two weeks wasn't much time, but we'd already given him the past month.

"After that, I'm not waiting around anymore. You can keep him as a plaything as long as he doesn't interfere with our lives anymore. Do we have an understanding?"

Thorn had been more than patient with me over Hunt. I'd accused Thorn of something hideous, and he still forgave me for it. I couldn't ask him to be patient any longer. My loyalty should be to him, my friend for the past ten years. "Yes, we have an understanding."

"Good." He rose to his feet and straightened his sleeves. "I'll see you later."

I left the couch and moved into his chest. I wrapped my arms around his waist and hugged him tightly, my face pressed right against his sternum. Thorn and I didn't hug often. Even when we were in public, affection was minimal. It made me realize I didn't show him much how much I cared about him as often as I should. "It'll always be us against the world."

His arms eventually moved around my shoulders,

and he rested his chin on my head. A quiet sigh escaped his lips. "I know, Titan."

---

I HAD THE ACCESS CODE TO HIS ELEVATOR, SO WE RODE it to the top floor of his building. Hunt told me I could come by anytime, so I took that offer seriously. The doors opened to his living room, where he had three large sofas situated around an enormous flat-screen TV.

He was sitting on the couch in just his sweatpants, his muscled chest chiseled and powerful. The light from the TV reflected against his tanned skin, high-lighting the endless grooves alone his trim waist. His hair was shaggy because he dried it with a towel the second he got out of the shower. A glass of amber liquid sat on the table in front of him, probably whiskey. He looked at us like he'd been expecting us even though he had no idea we were coming.

Whenever I looked at him, it always took me a moment to think of something to say. His handsome-ness blinded me, made me forget how to be in control. He was the only man in the world who made me want to submit, made want to be pinned down and lavished with endless kisses at the hollow of my throat and my shoulders. Those brown eyes were dark and brooding, but I found such beauty in that darkness. He stared at me like he didn't notice Thorn beside me. He made me feel like the only person in the room when we were surrounded by hundreds of people. "Is this a bad time?"

He rose to his full height, his physique stretching over me. He was the same height as Thorn, but he somehow felt like the tallest person in the room. His eyes were reserved for me, ignoring Thorn like he was insignificant. "There's never a bad time for you to visit." He took me in a moment longer, focusing on the tightness of my sweater across my chest. He glimpsed up to my neck, his eyes kissing me where his lips couldn't. After he was full of my appearance, he acknowledged Thorn by extending his hand.

Thorn eyed it and took nearly ten seconds before he reciprocated. He took a seat on one of the sofas, ignoring the baseball game on the screen.

Hunt didn't touch me, but it seemed like he wanted to. His eyes did all the touching, exploring my body through my clothes. The stare was searing, as if he was branding me like cattle.

"Thank you for talking to Thorn." I spoke with projected confidence. I could walk into a room with a dozen male executives and not flinch at their sexist comments and backhanded insults. But when Hunt was in front of me, I didn't feel like the badass woman who was taking over the world. I didn't feel like Titan —just Tatum.

"I wouldn't let you lose the most important person in your life. He's a good man. I sleep better at night knowing you have him."

I didn't glance at Thorn's expression to see his reaction, even though I was curious. I kept my eyes glued to the face I saw in my dreams. His chin had just been shaved, and he was nothing but smooth skin and chiseled bone structure. I wanted to run my kisses along that jawline, to enjoy him the way he wanted to enjoy me.

"I'm sorry I accused him in the first place. Just had to make sure." His arms remained by his sides, but I saw them shake slightly, like he wanted to grab me and pull me against his chest.

"Well...now you know."

Hunt sat down again, his flawless physique looking impeccable even in a seated position.

I didn't know where to sit. I felt an unspoken divide between the two men. I should sit beside Thorn, but I also wanted to sit beside Hunt. I moved to the third sofa and sat in the center, taking the neutral position. I crossed my legs and felt Hunt's ruthless stare all over my body.

Thorn leaned back into the cushions and rested his ankle on the opposite knee. "Titan and I had a long conversation about the three of us. We thought we would share it with you."

Hunt's eyes were still on me. "Alright."

"Titan and I have our future planned out. We both know exactly what we want, and everything was fine until you showed up." Thorn propped his elbow on the armrest with his fingertips resting against his temple. "Now everything is a mess, and we don't like it."

"I don't like it either." Hunt rested his elbows on his knees and leaned forward, his searing gaze reserved for me.

Thorn continued. "Titan and I think the evidence is overwhelming, but a small part of us thinks there's a possibility you're innocent."

He didn't blink. "I am innocent."

"We're going to give you a chance to prove it," I said. "You have two weeks to give us suitable evidence. But once the two weeks is over, that's it. Thorn and I are moving forward. We can't keep waiting around anymore."

His expression didn't change, but his anger slightly expanded in the room. "I'll do the best I can. But there's always the possibility that I can't find anything strong enough to exonerate me. You need to trust me, Titan. I know that's a lot to ask, but you need to have a little faith."

There were times when I couldn't believe he would ever do anything to hurt me. But when I remembered what had happened, I couldn't overlook it. "Those papers were sitting in your desk, Hunt. How can you expect me to believe you when I found them there?"

It was the first time he dropped his gaze, the disappointment heavy on his shoulders. "I already explained that."

"And your explanation wasn't good enough," I said calmly. "You hired someone to dig up everything they could on me. You had those papers at your disposal. After all that work, you really put those papers in your drawer and never looked at them?" I asked incredulously. "As much as I want to believe you, that's not a sufficient explanation for me."

"And me," Thorn added. "It's a strange coincidence that the exact same story was given to the newspapers under your name. Too much of a coincidence..."

I held Hunt's gaze and watched his jaw clench. "And then that woman—"

"It didn't happen," he said. "I dropped her off at

home. That's it." His eyes fired up with outrage. "Of all things, I need you to know I've always been faithful to you. There's only one woman on this planet that I want—and she's looking at me."

Now it was my turn to bow my head.

Thorn stepped in. "This is what I think. I think you originally had it out for Titan. She's a competitor, and you wanted to sabotage her. We all know how ambitious you are, Hunt. You got close to her, gained her trust, and then betrayed her. But in the process, you actually started to care about her. Fell in love with her. And now you're trying to undo everything you did in order to win her back. That's the only explanation I can think of. But if you really love her, you should just come clean about it. That way we'd know the truth and could decide how to move forward. I know Titan loves you. She might be able to forgive you and give you another chance if you just told her what really happened."

Hunt massaged his hands as he shook his head. "Even if she forgave me and gave me another chance, I still couldn't say that—because it's not true. I never betrayed her. And I will never betray her."

As always, my heart turned to mush inside my chest.

"If you're so certain I'm a traitor, why are you

giving me two weeks?" It was the first time Hunt looked at Thorn.

Thorn held Hunt's gaze with his fingertips still against his temple. "Just in case I'm wrong. I don't want Titan to lose the man she loves for no reason at all. And if you can't clear yourself, then she'll have the closure she needs to move on."

Hunt turned back to me, his shoulders not as broad as they usually were. He leaned back against the couch and released a heavy sigh. When he looked at me, his mind didn't seem to be there anymore. He appeared lost.

The three of us sat in tense silence as the minutes stretched on. Hunt covered his lips with his fingertips and looked across his living room but didn't focus on anything in particular. His eyes were heavy-lidded, and he seemed removed from the situation completely.

I watched him even though I didn't expect him to say anything more. If only I could read his mind, I would have all the answers I needed.

Thorn left the couch and walked out of the living room. "I'll leave you two alone." He hit the button on the wall and stepped into the elevator. The doors closed, and then the mechanism shifted as it began its descent.

Now, we were alone together, the TV playing quietly in the background.

Hunt grabbed the remote and turned it off.

Now it was just silent.

I could hear him breathe. He could probably hear me breathe too.

Now that Thorn was gone, Hunt looked at me again.

I stared back. We only sat this far away from each other when there were witnesses in the room. When it was just the two of us, it felt strange to be apart like this. He was on the other side of the living room, but it seemed like he was on another planet. The tension pulled at both of us, an invisible cord yanking us closer together.

Hunt patted his thigh, silently beckoning me to come to him.

I didn't move.

"Baby, come here," he whispered. "Or I'll walk over there and make you."

I'd just told him all the reasons why I didn't trust him, but I still wanted to cross that room and drop into his lap. I still wanted to be smothered with all those kisses. I wanted to tell him I loved him and listen to him say it back. I crossed the room and straddled his hips before I lowered myself to his lap.

His hands circled my waist, and he positioned me on top of him, getting me close to his chest. He stared into my face before he leaned in and pressed a soft kiss to my mouth, a kiss that was simple but filled with unspoken emotion. He kissed my upper lip before he pulled the bottom one into his mouth. He gave it a gentle tug before he released it.

I rested my forehead against his and closed my eyes. "I hate you..." The sudden emotion came from deep inside my chest. It came directly from my heart, the source of all my pain. "I hate that I love you. I hate the way you have this effect on me. I can't think straight when it comes to you. If you were anyone else, I would have turned my back a long time ago. But I'm still here because you have this power over me. I just want to be happy again. I want to have all the things we promised we would have. But I can't trust you. I hate that I can't trust you..."

He moved his lips to my temple and kissed me. "I don't have any power over you, Titan. The reason you're still here isn't just because you love me. It's because that brilliant brain of yours is telling you I'm the right man for you. It's telling you that I'm innocent. It perceives more than you can comprehend." His hand slid across my cheek to direct my gaze toward him. "I'll get the evidence that you need.

You'll see. And then you'll know that you were right."

———

I WALKED INTO THE CONFERENCE ROOM AT Stratosphere and saw Hunt standing near the window. He had an open folder in his hands, and he was reading something, his eyes shifting from left to right. In a black suit with a cream collared shirt underneath, he looked like he owned the whole city. Black was a great color on him. It complimented his dark eyes and hair. The tanned skin of his neck and knuckles only made the color look more stunning on him. I couldn't think of another man I found nearly as attractive. The men I'd slept with were all handsome and masculine, but Hunt was a completely different breed.

He set the folder on the table when he realized I was in the room. He greeted me with a look instead of words. Whenever we were alone together, we didn't have extensive conversations. We could communicate in silence and make our thoughts perfectly clear. Hunt was a pro at it.

I sat down and pulled my tablet out of my bag.

"I'm going to talk to Bruce Carol."

My eyes shifted up to him.

"I want you to come with me. If he admits anything, I want you to see for yourself. If he acts guilty, I want you to see that with your own eyes too."

"You're just going to walk in there and make an allegation like that?" I asked incredulously.

"Yep."

"Is there a more tactful way to do this?"

"No." He lowered himself into the chair across from me. "It's pretty simple. We're going to walk in and assume he's the one responsible. We'll say we know it's him and see what his reaction is. If it's not Thorn, I can't think of anyone else. Carol's our man."

"Should Thorn come along for this?"

"That's up to you."

Instead of looking at the report on my tablet, I stared at Hunt across from me. After Thorn left last night, Hunt and I hit the sheets, and he buried me in his bed. He pinned me down with his muscular body and took me slow and deep. My knees were positioned against my waist, and he hit me hard with every stroke. It was impossible to look at him without thinking about our sweaty bodies moving together.

And the way I'd said his name a dozen times.

"Let's do it tomorrow."

"Where?" I asked.

"He still has his apartment here in the city. We'll start there."

"Alright."

"Since he's unemployed, I say we hit him in the middle of the day. He won't expect it, and he won't have any company."

"His wife and kids," I noted.

"She left him. Took the kids with her."

"Ohh..." I didn't keep tabs on my old enemies. Bruce Carol would have gotten a much better deal if he hadn't insulted me like a pig. All he had to do was treat me with respect, and we could have had a strong business relationship. I shouldn't feel bad where he ended up—even though I did. I sympathized with his family, the ones who were punished because of his mistake.

"He'll be alone." He opened the folder he'd been examining and slid the first page toward me. "Should we start with this, or did you have something you'd like to discuss first?" Hunt respected my decision to remain professional while we were working, but that look he reserved only for me was always in his eyes. Even if he wanted to wipe it away, he probably couldn't.

And I wouldn't want him to.

I FINISHED A MEETING THAT WENT LONGER THAN I
anticipated, and Jessica had lunch waiting for me in
my office. It was a Cobb salad with dressing on the
side—along with a glass of water. I shouldn't let Hunt's
words get to me, but his concern wormed its way to my
heart. Hunt had the uncanny ability to get past all my
defenses when no one else could make a single dent.

I'd barely taken a few bites before Jessica spoke
into my intercom. "Titan, Mr. Hunt is here to see you."

I just saw him a few hours ago. Why did he need to
see me in person? If he needed something, he could
just send me a message. Even a phone call would be
fine. "Send him in."

"Yes, Titan."

I took a few more bites of my food since I didn't
need to impress Hunt. My desk could be a mess, and
my lunch could be all over the place. My favorite
drink, along with the entire decanter, could be there
too, and it wouldn't matter.

Jessica opened the door and ushered him inside.

I looked up and saw the brown eyes that occupied
my dreams, the eyes that looked into mine when he
was burying his desire between my legs every night.
But the appearance was slightly harsher, colder.

When I took in the rest of his appearance, I realized I wasn't looking at Hunt at all. This man had a similar appearance, with the same height, musculature, and facial expression. The same hard bones shaped his face, the same dark hair sat on top of his head. He was strong and lean, possessing natural power that filled every corner of the room. He was intimidating just by his appearance. He could make an entire speech without uttering a single word.

This wasn't Diesel Hunt.

It was Vincent Hunt.

Even if Jessica had clarified, I wouldn't have been prepared for this meeting. I probably wouldn't have agreed to see him and called Hunt instead. But now we were face-to-face, and there was nothing I could but meet his look head on.

In addition to Diesel's tales about his childhood, I knew Vincent Hunt was one of the most successful businessmen in the world. He was a self-made billionaire just the way I was. He stood on his own two feet and turned the path to gold. His interests exceeded our borders and reached all over the world. He had investments in foreign markets, factories overseas, and luxury resorts all over Europe. The only reason why I knew those things was because I watched my competitors as closely as I watched myself.

He stopped in front of my desk, wearing a light gray suit with a black tie. He was Hunt's height, so he exceeded mine by at least a foot. The look he gave me was nothing like the one his son gave me. He studied every inch of my face like a competitor. He sized me up as if we were going to battle.

I refused to be intimidated by anyone, especially the man who caused Hunt so much pain. I locked our gazes with my head held high, my shoulders back. I rose to my feet and regarded him coolly. "Mr. Hunt. It's a pleasure."

He shook my hand as he cracked a smile. It was handsome just the way Hunt's was. His jaw was free of hair, and he maintained a neat appearance. He must have been in his fifties, but he could easily pass for a much younger age. His hair was still dark, and judging from his looks, confidence, and wealth, he was probably still seeing women in their twenties. "No, Ms. Titan. The pleasure is entirely mine." He had a firm grip, ironclad but not suffocating. He pulled away and took a seat in the armchair facing my desk. His posture never slouched. His shoulders were broad and masculine, packed with muscle that hadn't deteriorated with age.

"You can call me Titan."

"Very well." He stared at me like he expected me to

lead the conversation even though he was the one who'd dropped by without an appointment.

If he were trying to play games with me, I wouldn't allow it to happen. I would sit there in silence until he spoke first. Jessica could cancel my schedule for the rest of the day if it came to that. I never walked away from a match unless I was the winner.

A hint of a smile stretched across his lips. "Your name suits you perfectly."

Damn right, it does.

"I have a business proposition for you."

There was no way this was a coincidence. Vincent Hunt and I had never met, and now he was in my office with a business opportunity. This had something to do with Diesel, and obviously, something to do with that interview he gave. I didn't know how Vincent Hunt connected me to his son, especially since they weren't on speaking terms. He must have figured it out on his own. "I'm listening."

"I'm a fan of Illuminance. As the biggest American cosmetics company, it's an enterprise that's never going to go out of business. Women will always want to look beautiful, and men will always want them to feel pressured to look beautiful. It's easy to mark up prices on something that everyone thinks they need." He was a smooth-talker, speaking eloquently and flawlessly. Diesel had the same attributes, and now I knew where he'd learned it from. Vincent Hunt had the same magnetic effect as his son. He owned the room—and he knew it.

But that was about to change. "You can skip the flattery, Mr. Hunt. I'm as knowledgeable about your business empire as you are about mine. We don't need to compare notes."

The corner of his mouth rose in a smile, amused rather than insulted. "I like a woman who gets right to the point."

My stoic expression didn't change, remaining as rigid as ever. He was charming with that nice smile and those expressive eyes.

"I want to be your distributor. I can get your products on every single shelf in the world. Not just China, Japan, and South Korea, but Russia, the Middle East, Eastern Europe, and everywhere else under the sun."

It was a goal I had in mind but hadn't reached. I'd arranged a meeting with Kyle Livingston just to explore China. Vincent Hunt exceeded my dreams by offering opportunities that would take decades to reach. But within the snap of a finger, he put the offer on the table. He was a wealthy man with decades of experience more than mine. He'd had the chance to establish business relationships long ago and maintain them to this day. I was young and still had my entire life ahead of me. That was one thing he would always have over me.

But instead of jumping out of my chair in excitement or cracking a smile, I remained hesitant. Vincent Hunt wouldn't offer this unless he wanted something in return. "Your terms?"

"Five percent of all profits in those territories."

Five percent was exceptionally low. Even though I managed a multibillion-dollar empire, five percent wasn't worth all the work he would have to do to make this happen. Even if he delegated it to his team, it would still be time-consuming. "And?"

"That's it. Five percent."

There was no point in negotiating a lower number because that was far below what I expected. Red flags were popping up all over my brain. It would be easy for him to develop his own cosmetics company and invade those retailers. Why help me and gain such little in return?

I had no idea—but it wasn't good.

The devil was sitting in front of me, and he offered me a deal any sane person couldn't refuse. He wanted something from me, something that I couldn't discern. All I could think of was Diesel.

This had something to do with him.

Going into business with Vincent Hunt would be a betrayal of my relationship with Diesel. It was a major conflict of interest and an insult. After everything Vincent put him through, it would be wrong for me to shake his hand.

But he was giving me everything I wanted.

I still didn't know how honest Diesel Hunt really was. I found those documents in his drawer, my most terrifying secret stacked into a pretty folder. Whether he really read them or not, he'd invaded my privacy. He wasn't entirely truthful, and there were so many caution signs everywhere.

Could I walk away from a deal like this for a man I didn't trust?

Could I walk away from billions?

Vincent hardly blinked as he stared at me. "I have to say, I'm surprised you aren't jumping out of your chair to shake my hand on this deal."

"I have to say, I'm surprised you offered such a deal. It's suspicious to me."

"We both make money. Nothing to be suspicious about."

That was bullshit. He had a trick up his sleeve. I didn't know what his motives were, but they weren't good.

"I'll give you the day to think about it." He rose to

his feet, towering over me once more. "But not much longer than that. I'm sure Kyle Livingston would be thrilled by the offer."

If Vincent Hunt swooped up Kyle, then I would be left with nothing. Kyle was my ticket into Asia, and without him, I had no hope for expansion. Something told me Vincent knew that, and he was using that to light a fire under my ass. It was a veiled threat. Vincent did his homework, knew exactly what my goals were so he could use them against me. He was doing everything possible to make sure I took this deal.

But why?

I rose out of my chair and walked around the desk. "Thank you. You'll hear from my office by tomorrow afternoon." I walked up to him, slightly unnerved that he looked so similar to the man I loved. I shook his hand, feeling the similarities in their grip and strength. Their knuckles were prominent in the same way, the veins from his forearms moving over the top of his hand just the way Diesel's did.

He dropped his hand and gave me a slight nod. "I hope you make the right decision, Titan. A deal like this only happens once in a lifetime." He stopped before he reached the door to turn around and look at me. "And most of the time, it doesn't happen at all."

## 13

I GOT the information from my PI. I knew exactly where Bruce Carol was staying. His penthouse was on the market, and he was waiting for it to sell before he packed up and headed somewhere else. He probably had enough in savings to live out a quiet retirement, but he wouldn't have enough to keep his yachts, luxury cars, and planes.

Too bad.

I got out of the shower after hitting the gym. I styled my hair and pulled on a pair of dark jeans and a long-sleeved shirt. I wasn't staying home tonight. My woman was at her penthouse, probably waiting for me to step out of the elevator doors at any moment. Instead of being home alone, I'd rather be naked and sweaty in her bed. I'd always been a sexual person who needed it on a regular basis, but with Titan, it wasn't about sex. It was much more than that—to both of us. It was when I felt most connected to her, and nothing else existed outside the four walls that surrounded us.

I had just pulled on my shoes when the elevator lit up and the doors opened.

Titan stepped inside, still in the black dress she'd been wearing at Stratosphere. Her stilettos were five inches tall and made her toned calves looked even sexier. She wore the uncomfortable shoes every single day but never broke her graceful stride.

My eyes quickly roamed over her body, seeing the tight fabric stretch across her perfect rack and her tiny waist. She was petite, but that fiery presence made her appear ten feet tall. The second I reached her, my hands glided around her hips until I felt the steep curve in her back, one of the features that aroused me the most. My head angled down to hers, and I gave her a kiss that was packed with the lustful thoughts I'd had about her all day. I had to sit across from her in a conference room fully clothed and discuss business while I fought the raging hard-on in my suit. My hands held her against me, allowing me to claim all of her mouth. Innocent kisses always turned devilish in nature. We couldn't touch without it developing into something more. We couldn't even look at each other without wanting to strip one another down to our basest nakedness. That was why I didn't want to let her go. I didn't want to search the world for her replacement. There was only one person in the world who affected me so deeply. I had to fight for her, to make sure I got to have this special joy for the rest of my life.

She ended the embrace before it could ignite into a wildfire. Her hands were against my chest, and they slowly drifted down to my hard stomach. "I want to see Bruce Carol tonight."

With lidded eyes and thoughts only on sex, I had to take a few seconds to digest what she said. "We agreed to see him in the morning."

"I don't want to wait." Her hands dropped from my stomach and returned to her sides.

My eyes shifted back and forth as I looked into hers. "Why?"

She held my expression, but there was an ounce of anxiousness in the look. She was unsteady, even desperate. "Because I need this answer, Hunt. I don't want to wait anymore."

The second I saw her step into my penthouse, there was only one thing I wanted to do. I wanted her face down and her ass up. I wanted to nail her from behind, to shove my thick cock inside that slick pussy until she was stuffed with my arousal. But Titan always got what she wanted—because I allowed her to. "Alright."

"Let's go." She turned back to the elevator and hit the button.

I pulled my jacket over my shoulders and looked into her face. "Everything alright?"

She watched the doors open with a distinct look of sadness on her face. "No, Hunt. Everything isn't alright. It hasn't been alright in a long time."

———

WE STEPPED ONTO HIS FLOOR AND APPROACHED his door.

"Let me do the talking."

She nodded.

I knocked on the door and waited for a response. Coming at night wasn't the best time. He could be drinking, drowning in his self-pity. When there wasn't an answer, I rang the doorbell. "Open up, Bruce."

A moment later, the door opened. Bruce Carol looked exactly the way he had a few months ago, but there were a few more lines on his face. His eyes were filled with unmistakable depression. He looked at me coldly, but the look he gave Titan was pure venom. "If you're here to gloat, you're wasting your time. You can't make me feel worse than I already do." He kept one hand on the door as if he was prepared to slam it in our faces.

Now he was my number-one suspect. He had the perfect motive to do this to us. We ruined his life, and now he wanted to do the same to us. "I know you're the one who went to the *New York Times* about Titan's story. I understand you're upset, but that was unnecessary."

"Went to the *New York Times*?" Bruce asked incredulously, his speech slightly slurred. "About that punk ex-boyfriend of hers?"

Titan didn't show the slightest reaction.

"I didn't tell anybody anything. I didn't know a damn thing about Titan before I met her. The only reason why I didn't want to work with her is because she looks like she has a tampon stuffed up her ass."

I didn't think twice before I crowded him with my fist raised.

Titan grabbed me by the arm and jerked me back. "He's not worth it. I've had worse things said about me, and I don't lose any sleep over it." She released me, still maintaining her proud look. "Ignore him."

Bruce stared at her, a look of contempt on his face.

"Don't you two have a business to run? Why are you here?"

He was beyond buzzed or just stupid. "I want to know why you did it. Why did you tell the newspapers about Titan? What were you trying to achieve? I can't sue you for defamation because it's accurate. There's nothing I can take away from you because you already lost everything. So you may as well enjoy the last bit of your revenge and tell us why you did it. Were you hoping Titan and I would no longer be partners? Titan is smarter than that. She knows I wouldn't betray her."

Bruce switched his gaze back to me, still wearing the exact same look of annoyance he'd been wearing since the very beginning of the conversation. "Like I said, I didn't tell anybody anything. What's the point of revenge when it doesn't change anything? My wife is gone, my kids won't speak to me... The only thing I enjoy is a good drink after a long day of selling all of my personal assets to pay my debt. Now, if you'll excuse me..." He stepped back inside his penthouse and shut the door. The bolt locked into place when he turned the knob. A second later, his footsteps tapped against the floor as he retreated farther inside his home.

I stared at the dark wood of the door because I

couldn't think. I had been certain this conversation would go differently. I had been certain if I seemed confident in my accusation, he would crack. Perhaps he knew Titan and I had issues between us, and by keeping the truth from us, we had to function in the dark. She didn't know if she could trust me, and that was exactly what he wanted. He was stupid for crossing us, but he wasn't quite as stupid as we both believed.

I bowed my head as the sigh left my lungs. My hands dragged down my face, and the frustration cracked through my bones. I was dismayed, disappointed, and furious. If I'd gotten the answers I wanted, Titan would be in my arms right now. But now we were just as distant as we were before—if not more.

I finally turned my head and looked at her.

Her expression hadn't changed. She turned away from the door and stepped farther into the hallway, the diamond necklace around her throat sparkling under the lamps that hung from both sides of the corridor.

I walked with her back down the hall, trailing away from his entryway where we couldn't be overheard. "He's lying."

She hit the button, and we both stepped inside the

elevator. We shifted down to the lobby level, the lights telling us exactly what floor we were on as we descended. She crossed her arms over her chest, her beautiful hair perfect around her shoulders.

"Baby, he's lying."

The only response I got her was a sigh.

I turned my head in her direction. "He's the only one with the motive."

"But he's lost everything, Hunt. He has no reason to lie anymore. If he wanted to tear us down, he would be gloating right now. But he seems nothing but indifferent."

"He's the only person it could possibly be."

"I want to believe you, Hunt. Believe me, I do. I've been patient. I've waited for you to give me a way to exonerate you. But it's not coming...and it's never going to come."

"Don't say that."

"It's true," she whispered.

I panicked as we stood side by side in the elevator. My life was stressful because of the enormity of my responsibilities, but I'd never been scared like this before. The most important thing in the world was about to be taken away from me. Just as I took away Bruce's legacy, he was going to take away the one thing that made me happy.

The elevator stopped on the ground floor, and we walked through the lobby to the back seat of my Mercedes. The divider was up, so the driver couldn't hear or see us. We headed back to my penthouse a few streets away.

Titan looked out the window, ignoring me as much as she could.

I stared out the other window, unsure how I was going to get out of this mess. The situation was so fucked up, and I couldn't blame Titan for feeling hesitant. If the situations were reversed, I'd have a hard time believing her too.

But I couldn't let him win.

I couldn't let him rip us apart.

"Just because I can't prove my innocence doesn't mean I'm guilty."

She kept her eyes out the window.

"Baby."

She wouldn't look at me.

"Titan." My hand moved to her thigh. "Look at me."

She watched the neon signs flash by before she finally turned her gaze on me. There was anger in her eyes, bubbling under the surface. She didn't hide her resentment, her obvious disappointment.

"I'm going to need you to believe me, Titan. I know it's a lot to ask, but you have to have faith in me."

She shook her head slightly. "It's too much to ask."

"You know I didn't do it."

"Hunt, I have no idea what to believe. I think it could go either way."

"You know I love you. That's something you have to believe in. I wouldn't have told the world about my relationship with my father if that wasn't true. I wouldn't have defended you from Bruce Carol if you didn't mean everything to me. I wouldn't have put you back together with Thorn, the man you're planning to marry, if I didn't put you first. Ignore the bad and focus on the good."

She turned back to the window, her lips pursed tightly together. "I think Thorn is right. And I also think you're right."

That just left me confused.

"I think you do love me. I think you would do anything for me. But I think your initial motives were evil. I think you wanted to tear me down, but in the process, you fell for me. Now you've been trying to make up for it."

It was a devastating blow, but I was also grateful that she knew I really cared about her. "That's not what happened, Titan."

"There's no evidence to suggest otherwise."

"I know...but I really am innocent."

She kept her gaze out the window, shutting me out. "I don't want to talk about this anymore, Hunt. I just want to move on."

I felt the finality of her tone fill the back seat of the car. I felt her pull away from me even though she didn't move. I felt her slip from my fingertips no matter how hard I was gripping her. The one person I loved more than anyone on this planet didn't trust me, didn't believe me. An invisible wall formed between us, and it was so solid I would never be able to get through. I wanted to scream until she heard me. I wanted to destroy everything in my path until she listened to me.

But there was nothing I could do.

Nothing at all.

## 14

"Everything alright?" Thorn was bare-chested and barefoot, just wearing his sweatpants. It was almost eleven in the evening, so it was much later than I would normally stop by. He walked up to me at the doorway, his hair flat because he didn't style it after he got out of the shower.

"Do you have company right now?"

"She left thirty minutes ago." He stood in front of me with his strong build, eyeing me with the same look of protective concern he'd been giving me the past decade. It was the look a brother would give a sister, but it was also the look a husband would give a wife. Sometimes I wondered how we had so much love between us, but not an ounce of it was romantic. Over all the years I'd known him, I'd never felt a single ounce of jealousy for the women he brought home.

But when I saw Hunt kiss that woman in the photograph, I thought I would never feel happiness again.

"Vincent Hunt stopped by my office today."

Thorn's eyes widened instantly. "What did he say? Did he talk about Diesel?"

"Never mentioned him. He gave me a business proposition."

His surprise immediately turned to suspicion. His eyes narrowed on my face, and he crossed his arms over my chest. "Out of the blue?"

"Yeah."

"You've never even met him before."

"I know."

Thorn shared the same healthy skepticism I did. Anytime anyone did anything, I always questioned it. I needed to understand someone's motives before I could trust them. Business was all about getting the best deal. If someone handed you something wonderful without expecting anything in return, that was just strange. Everyone was selfish. Everyone had their own self-interests—me included. "What was his offer?"

"He said he would get my products into retailers all over the world, not just China. And in exchange, he wants five percent of profits."

Thorn's eyes widened again. "What?"

"Yeah..."

"Five percent?" he asked incredulously. "That's insane. The bare minimum he should be asking is twenty percent—and even that's a little low."

"I know. He said I had until tomorrow to think it over. And if my answer is no, he's going to offer the deal to Kyle Livingston."

"Who's your contact to get into China..."

"Yeah."

Thorn was fiercely intelligent and connected the dots the second they were drawn. He shifted his weight to the other foot then rubbed his jaw. "His offer sounds too good to be true."

"I thought the same thing."

"It's an incredible opportunity. If Kyle had the offer on the table, he would have taken it in a heartbeat."

"I know."

"I don't see any downside to this...which concerns me. It doesn't seem like Vincent Hunt is getting much out of this...just a partnership with you."

I didn't see any advantage for him either. The fact that he threw Kyle Livingston into the situation told me he was doing everything he could to make sure I said yes. "It seems like he wants me more than the partnership."

"Exactly. It must have something to do with Diesel."

"I agree."

"Does he know about the two of you?"

"I don't think so. Hunt wouldn't have told him. They don't speak."

"Could he have found out some other way?"

"I don't think so," I answered. "But Hunt went to the media about their relationship the second the newspapers talked about my past with Jeremy. Vincent probably figured out the two instances were related, that Hunt was trying to bury my story and get me out of the spotlight."

"So he knows you mean something to him."

"But he must know I'm seeing you."

"Maybe he just thinks Hunt is fond of you, then," he said. "Maybe he thinks you're good friends. You are doing business together." Thorn rubbed his chin as he considered all of this. "Maybe this is an attack on Diesel. He wants to sabotage your relationship and partnership."

"Maybe…"

"He doesn't care about the money at all. He just wants to give you something you desperately want so it'll be a betrayal of Hunt. Maybe he has more plans, like persuading you that Diesel isn't a good guy."

"That's the only thing that makes sense."

"But whatever his reason is, you have to take that offer."

I nearly did a double take. I looked into Thorn's face and realized he was being dead serious. "What?"

"Titan, this is exactly what you want." He dropped his arms to his sides, the excitement entering his limbs. "It's even better than what Kyle Livingston can offer you. Vincent Hunt is one of the wealthiest people in the world, and he doesn't do business with just anyone. You're opening the door to untapped potential. This is huge. This is big for both of us. You'll move up on the *Forbes* list within a year, and once we're married, we're going to skyrocket to the top."

It was exactly what I wanted, but I couldn't share the same enthusiasm. "Thorn, I can't do that to Diesel."

"You're joking, right?"'

My Hunt and his father would never get along. They were sworn enemies. They weren't even family. They just looked alike in appearance, but they had nothing in common underneath the skin. "Not because I'm sleeping with him. He's my partner. He's my friend."

"It's just business, Titan. It doesn't have to effect Stratosphere. You don't even need to talk about it."

"It'll definitely come up."

"And he's the one who betrayed you first, in case you've forgotten. He sold your story to the entire world. He had your files in his desk drawer. Let's not sugarcoat his crimes just because you're in love with him."

After our conversation with Bruce Carol, I believed Hunt's innocence even less. "We talked to Bruce Carol tonight. That didn't go anywhere. He denied everything."

"Of course he did," Thorn said. "Because Hunt is the one who did it. I wouldn't be surprised if Hunt regrets it and is a different guy now. But he can't take back what he did, and the fact that he won't just own up to it makes it worse. Men admit their mistakes. And men learn from them."

I bowed my head so I could take in his words. There was no going back now. Hunt's loyalty would always be questioned. I couldn't trust him, and neither could Thorn. I could enjoy him as much as I wanted, but I had to shut off the possibility we could ever be anything more. Thorn was my future. He was the only person I could truly count on.

"You don't owe him anything, Titan."

I would be stupid not to take Vincent Hunt's offer. It was a great deal that I wouldn't find anywhere else.

To make matters worse, if I didn't take it, Kyle Livingston would reap all the rewards. It would make it a million times harder to reach my goal.

"You're taking this deal, Titan. Another opportunity like this isn't going to come up."

"I know..."

"Then say yes. Meet with him tomorrow and say yes." He gave me a harder stare, turning aggressive. Thorn was brutal when it came to business. It was one of his many strengths, turning into a ruthless opponent until he got what he wanted. He was the perfect person to have on my side of the ring. "You'll regret it if you don't. Don't let another man hold you back. Don't let another man take something away from you, Titan. This is yours. You earned it."

———

WHEN I ENTERED MY PENTHOUSE, HUNT WAS SITTING ON the couch. He was in the same clothes he'd been wearing earlier that evening. After seeing Carol, the car had pulled up to my penthouse, and I got out without saying a word to him.

He didn't follow me.

But now he was here, leaning forward with his elbows resting on his thighs.

I hung my jacket on the coatrack and slipped off my heels.

He rose to his feet and walked toward me, wearing a mask of restrained anger. The conversation with Bruce Carol didn't reveal anything besides Hunt's guilt. There was nothing that could save us now. There was no hope for either one of us. We needed to move on with our lives. I had a destiny to fulfill, and so did he.

His deep brown eyes moved to my face, and they were much gentler than his father's. While they were hard and authoritative, they retained a distinct soft-ness that his father didn't possess. I assumed he got that from his mother—a woman I never met. "I know you don't want to talk about it anymore. I don't want to talk about it either."

I was disappointed in Hunt for doing this to us. I'd found a man I loved with all my heart, but now I had to shut down all my emotions, never to let them emerge again. My life would go back to what it was before, just sex, work, and Thorn. I had to accept the fact that Hunt was my enemy at some point, even if I believed he really loved me now. I couldn't forgive that kind of treachery.

"I just want to be with you."

Conversations were exhausting, especially when

they were repetitive. The pain in my chest had no effect on my desire for this man. I wanted him as much as I ever had. I wanted to get lost in the lust that swept over both of us. I didn't want to think about tomorrow or the future that lay ahead. For now, I just wanted to slip away into another world—to a place where I didn't have to think.

My hands slid up his chest and to his shoulders, and I pushed the black jacket off his body and onto the floor. I moved onto my tiptoes and pressed my mouth to his, feeling the stubble that had started to grow back. "Then be with me."

He took the invitation greedily and devoured me insatiably. He moved his hand into my hair, and he wrapped his other arm around my waist so he could lift me into his body. He carried me into my bedroom before he dropped me onto the mattress. Clothes came off, and shoes were kicked away. After a lightning-quick strip, he was on top of me, all over me, and deep between my legs.

The world felt right again.

He breathed against my mouth as he shoved himself inside me, sliding through my slickness until there was no room left for him. His hand anchored into my hair, and he took me with powerful thrusts, fucking me without a hint of gentleness.

My fingers slid into his hair then clawed down his neck to his shoulders. I clung to him and locked my ankles together, feeling him ram me farther into the mattress. Sweat smeared across our skin. Our pants turned to moans. Our moans turned to screams. My nails scratched his skin until I nearly broke through and drew blood.

Hours passed, and we kept moving together, reaching our mutual pleasure before we started over again. Not a word was said. Only moans and breaths were shared. The trust that I once adored between was long gone, but the passion would never die. It was uncontrollable, unquenchable. It was something that would always bring us together—time and time again.

---

I FELT DECEITFUL NOT TELLING HUNT ABOUT THE DEAL I was about to take from his father.

But it was business, and my business was none of his concern. He didn't tell me about his other companies, ever share insights into things he encountered. I did the same because there was no reason to discuss it. We were only involved because of Stratosphere. Outside of that, there was nothing to discuss.

But I felt terrible anyway.

I felt like I was hiding something from a friend. Withholding information from someone I cared about. Thorn was right in his argument, but no amount of logic would sway the guilty feelings inside me.

Jessica spoke through the intercom. "I have Mr. Hunt on line one."

Now that I had two different men in that family to deal with, she needed to be more specific. "From now on, include the first name as well."

"Of course, Titan. It's Vincent Hunt."

I was hoping it was Diesel instead. But I knew Vincent would expect his answer before three o'clock. I stared at the light on the receiver before I picked up the phone and took the call. "Hello, Mr. Hunt." It felt strange to address his father by the same name I addressed Diesel in public. They had the same last name, but they were nothing alike.

"Titan, it's great to hear your voice. I hope we can meet to finalize the contract later this week. I can only assume your answer is yes."

I'd have to be stupid to say no.

Thorn was right about everything. I didn't owe Diesel anything. He'd betrayed me. Just because he regretted it later didn't excuse his actions. He couldn't be trusted, and I had to do the right thing for myself as well as Thorn. Not taking this deal would hurt me in the end. Just because Vincent had a personal vendetta against his son didn't mean I should be concerned about it. Diesel might end up resigning from Stratosphere, and that would only work out in my favor. "I've thought a lot about it. Sounds like a great opportunity."

"That's wonderful to hear. I'm glad you're on board." He even sounded like Diesel, just a little older. He carried the conversation in the same way, had a masculine tone that was deep and profound.

Something in my gut tightened. The guilt ate away at me. I pictured Diesel's face once he knew about this deal. I knew he would be hurt, not because his own father was out to hurt him, but because I took his offer.

That would hurt him most of all.

I pictured that hard face softening in a vulnerable way. The way his chin dropped slightly as he moved his gaze to the floor. I pictured the disappointment in his eyes, the kind of heartbreak he rarely showed.

That's when I knew I couldn't do it. Even though Diesel had hurt me, I couldn't hurt him.

I couldn't hurt the man I loved.

Even if I had every right to. "I really appreciate the offer, Mr. Hunt. I think it's a great opportunity, and I'm flattered you extended the invitation to me. However, I have to decline."

Silence.

Long, heavy silence.

Hostile tension.

"Kyle Livingston is a great partner to have. He's as familiar with this space as I am. I think he'll be a great partner to take on."

He still didn't say a single word.

I'd never heard someone sound so livid without uttering a syllable.

Finally, he spoke. "That's too bad, Titan. A shame."

I could feel all the anger, all the rage. He kept himself composed and polite, but there was no masking his complete disappointment. He was certain I would say yes because I'd have to be stupid to say no. He never saw this coming.

I didn't see it coming either. Thorn would be pissed. I knew I would regret this later. Diesel didn't deserve my loyalty when he hadn't been as loyal to me. But something in my heart stopped me from crossing the line. The last thing I ever wanted to do was hurt Diesel.

Because I loved him with all my heart. "Take care, Mr. Hunt."

"You too, Titan."

I<small>F WE WEREN'T IN A PUBLIC RESTAURANT,</small> T<small>HORN WOULD</small> scream.

Which is why I purposely told him at lunch.

"You said no?" He kept his voice low, but he couldn't keep his tone under control. "You've gotta be fucking kidding me."

Our plates were in front of us, and we'd both eaten most of our green salads. A basket of bread was in between us, but we'd each only had a single slice. "It didn't feel right, Thorn." I wanted to apologize, but I didn't owe him an apology. It was my business, not his.

He shook his head, his jaw clenched so tight it seemed like it would snap in two. "I hate that asshole. Ever since he came into our lives, it's been a goddamn circus." He rubbed his temple like it was all he could do without flipping the table over.

"I'll find another way. Based on what Hunt described, his father doesn't seem like someone I want to do business with anyway."

"Because he treated Brett like shit?" he asked incredulously. "That has nothing to do with his business. That's his own issue. That's like saying you aren't a good business partner because you drink like a horse at a trough."

"Not the same thing…"

"It is the same thing," he hissed. "This was a great opportunity for us, and you blew it."

"For me," I corrected. "This is my business. I don't interfere with your business decisions."

"But we're going to be one entity very soon, Titan. Your wealth affects my wealth. That's one of the reasons we agreed to do this in the first place. You only said no because of Hunt, despite everything he's done to you. How can your judgment be so impaired?"

"I know it's hard to understand, but I couldn't do it. I couldn't live with that decision."

He rolled his eyes and threw his napkin on the table. "Unbelievable…"

"Vincent Hunt isn't the only way to get what I want. I assure you, I'll figure it out."

"Or you could have just taken the easier route."

I ignored the comment. "Let's just move forward."

"Can we?" he asked incredulously. "Hunt is still a problem."

"No, he's not. He's just a guy I screw. I don't want anything else from him."

Thorn's jaw hadn't unclenched yet. "You've said that before…"

"I mean it this time. He knows that. We've come to a dead end, and we can't move forward anymore. I can't trust him, and he knows he can't convince me otherwise. It is what it is."

"If that's true, why didn't you take the deal?"

It might be too complicated for him to understand. "Hunt and I do have something now. It isn't much, but we are friends. We are business partners. I don't think he would ever betray me again. That's enough for me to remain loyal to him. I don't have any urge to hurt him, to get revenge for what he did to me. I know my love for him clouds my thoughts...but I still wouldn't change my decision."

Thorn was still angry, but he slowly drifted back down to calm. My decision was final, and there was nothing he could say to reserve it, so he accepted it. The tightness in his jaw released, and he finally looked at me again. "He's a very lucky man to have the love of a woman like you. Hope he appreciates it someday."

I grabbed a piece of bread and tore off the edge before I placed it in my mouth. I needed something to do with my hands, something to deflect the intimate observation he'd just made.

Thorn must have known he made me uncomfortable because he changed the subject. "I was thinking of proposing this Saturday. I'd gather all our friends and family to a nice dinner, and once they bring out the dessert, I'd get down on one knee. What do you think?"

I refused to think about Hunt. That possibility was long gone. Now he was just a friend and business partner, someone who fulfilled my fantasies behind closed doors. I wiped him from my thoughts and looked at the man I was going to spend my life with, the man who'd always been there for me. He would be the father of my children, the man who stood beside me when my body was no longer beautiful and I was frail and old. We'd be buried together, our ashes becoming part of the earth. Hunt could be in my life as long as he wanted to be, but he would never be anything more than a secret. "I think it's a great idea."

Thorn's anger was gone, and a smile replaced his previous frown. "Perfect. I'll make the arrangements."

## 15

My LIFE SEEMED to hit a brick wall.

The path I wanted to take was blocked. There was no way around it. All I could do was turn around and go back the way I came. I'd have to settle for being Titan's bedmate. I could be the only man in her life between the sheets—but I would never have anything more.

She'd give everything else to Thorn—her husband.

I wasn't the kind of man who ever gave up, but I didn't see any way out of this mess. All of my leads turned into nothing. I had no evidence to prove my innocence. Titan wanted to believe me, but she just couldn't. For a woman who had already suffered so much, I didn't blame her from refraining from taking a risk.

She'd already taken too many risks.

My only hope was that she would change her mind somewhere down the road, that she would realize my soul wasn't capable of such a betrayal. We were both broken people with no one to trust. If only we could trust each other, we would have everything we needed.

I sat at my desk with my cheek propped against my fingertips. My computer screen went black twenty minutes ago from inactivity, and the messages sitting on my desk hadn't received a response.

I was too distracted to do anything.

Natalie spoke through the intercom. "I have Mr. Hunt for you."

This time, I knew it wasn't Jax. It was my father, and this time, he would have a more concrete threat to throw at me. But he could do his worst. I didn't give a damn anymore. "Put him through."

"Yes, sir."

I picked up the phone and pressed it to my ear. I leaned back in the leather chair and looked at the view of skyscrapers that surrounded my building. Since I already lost the one thing that mattered to me, it didn't seem like my father could do any more damage. "How can I help you?" I sounded authoritative, as usual. But I didn't show anger or hatred. It was unfortunate that my relationship with my father had turned into such a petty war. If only he knew I'd betrayed him to keep the woman I loved, things might be different. But then again, he was the least compassionate man I've ever known. He wouldn't give a damn.

"I find it ironic that a man so disloyal has the loyalty of the most powerful woman in this city."

It only took me two seconds to break that code. He was referring to Titan. But what exactly he was referring to was a mystery to me. I couldn't ask too many questions. Otherwise, it would make me seem incompetent. Titan hadn't mentioned my father, so I didn't know what kind of interaction they had. "I am loyal—to the right people."

"I raised you into the man you are today. I put you in the finest schools on the East Coast. I trained you to be smart, cunning, and powerful. I put food on the table to keep you full. Everything you ever needed, I provided. I deserve your loyalty more than anyone else." I could feel the sparks from his heat, feel his tension as it rose. I could hear the rage—as well as the pain.

"You betrayed Mom the second you kicked Brett out. Now that's disloyal." We'd never spoken of it since the day I'd turned my back on him. The rare times we saw each other across the room there was only an exchange of hostile looks. After a decade of silence, we were finally talking about it. Although, I had no idea how it related to Titan.

"He was never my son."

"You should have loved him like he was." Defending Brett had cost me years of heartache with my father. I hated this animosity that we both felt for one another. But standing up for my brother was the right thing to do. My mother would have wanted me to be there for Brett. "And you shouldn't have outcaste your oldest son for ten years because of it."

"Outcaste you?" he asked coldly. "You're the one who turned your back on me, Diesel. Let's not rewrite history."

"Because you forced my hand. You gave me no other choice." When I woke up this morning, the last thing I'd expected was to have this conversation with my father. I didn't expect to explore the underlying anger we both felt. "Titan is loyal because I'm loyal to her. That's how it goes, Vincent. It's a two-way street." I still couldn't figure out how she fit into the conversation, but asking bluntly would only make me look stupid.

"A businesswoman of her standing doesn't say no to a deal like that out of loyalty. It has to be something far stronger. I'll never figure out how you earned the love of an incredible woman like her. You're a very lucky man."

---

THE CONVERSATION WAS TOO INTIMATE FOR ME TO STOP by her office. I could call her, but that didn't seem right either. I waited in her living room, knowing it was the first place she would go once she was off work.

After five, she stepped inside the apartment. She removed her jacket and placed her satchel on the end table next to the door. When she realized I was there, she didn't show a hint of a surprise.

I walked toward her and didn't spot anything different on her face. She seemed to be exactly the same, a little tired after a long day at the office.

She didn't need to look up as high because her heels gave her an extra five inches of height. She leaned into me and gave me a quick kiss on the lips, greeting me exactly the way I liked when no one was around. "You need to stop dropping by like this, Hunt."

"I know. But I need to talk to you."

"What's up?" It still seemed like everything was the same, like she hadn't spoken to my father recently.

"My father called me today."

Once he was mentioned, her stoic expression softened. Her thoughts became more visible, more readable.

"He said I'm lucky to have your loyalty. What does that mean?"

She didn't panic at the question, but she became uncomfortable. She shifted her weight to a different leg and crossed her arms over her chest, stalling as she considered a good response to the question. She clearly knew exactly what I was talking about.

"Titan."

"He stopped by my office the other day and made me a business offer."

Why didn't it surprise me that he would do that? "What was the offer?"

"He said he would get me into stores all over the world and would only take five percent of my profits."

That was a horrible deal for him, but he wasn't after the money.

"I told him I needed to think about it for a day. He said if I turned it down, he would give it to Kyle Livingston instead."

So he'd basically threatened her.

She sighed before she continued. "But I said no. I

could tell he was angry, but he didn't make a fuss about it."

Expanding Illuminance was Titan's biggest goal. She wanted to get her products everywhere, expand her already successful business. It's what she needed Kyle Livingston for, and it would be easy for my father to make all her dreams come true. Saying no couldn't have been easy. After what she thought I did to her, she would have been entitled to say yes. But she didn't.

She said no.

"I know he was trying to take a swipe at you. Maybe he thought he could turn me against you. Maybe he thought it would hurt you. I'm not sure. But I didn't want to go through with it, so I didn't." She downplayed it like her decision wasn't a big deal, but it was a very big deal.

I was a man of few words, but now I had even less to say. Her actions left me speechless, and I couldn't express a single emotion. Anyone else would have taken that deal, no matter how much it hurt me. Even my closest friends would be tempted by it. Titan was a powerful woman with high ambitions. The opportunity could have taken her to a new level. Instead, she cared more about me.

What could I possibly say to that?

"Titan..." I took a deep breath as I looked at her,

overcome with pain and joy. The most amazing woman in the world loved me, and she would never understand how much I loved her. She was standing right in front of me, but I couldn't really touch her. I could never really have her. "I...I don't know what to say."

"You don't need to say anything, Hunt."

"But I do need to say something. That was... There are no words. You could have taken that deal, and no one would have judged you for it. You chose to be loyal to me...even though you think I'm a liar."

Her gaze shifted to the floor. "My love for you blinds me...I know."

"It doesn't blind you," I whispered. "Your instincts are right, Titan. You don't even realize how right you are." I moved my hands to her arms, and I gently caressed her up and down.

She tilted her chin up and looked at me, her eyes full of the affection that never died away. "Thorn was so angry at me..."

"I don't blame him. My father is an asshole, but he's good at what he does. It would have been a great opportunity."

She nodded slightly. "I couldn't live with the decision, knowing it would hurt you so much. I never want to hurt you."

My hands automatically squeezed her, and I pressed my forehead to hers. I felt the passionate connection between us, the unbreakable hold that kept us close together. Nothing could tear us apart— not the lies, and not my father. "I know. I never want to hurt you either, baby." I kissed her forehead, feeling my heart ache because of her pain. If only she understood just how loyal I was to her, how much I'd always been loyal. All of this pain she harbored would be gone. She would know I was the perfect partner to spend her life with, even better than Thorn.

She took a deep breath when she felt me kiss her. She suddenly slipped away, removing herself from my grasp like she didn't want to be touched any longer. Something I said had pushed her away. Or something she felt made her put a wall between us. "Thorn is going to ask me to marry him on Saturday."

Just when I felt a surge of hope, it was taken away from me. Just when I felt a connection with her, it was severed. I was in pain all over again, getting close to the fire but then being jerked back into the cold.

"I'm going to say yes. And there's nothing you can do to change my mind."

I WAS RUNNING OUT OF OPTIONS.

If she became engaged to Thorn, it wasn't a death blow. But it would make it a lot harder for her to leave him and be with me—publicly. I'd already spoken to Titan about it countless times, and I couldn't change her mind. Her heart believed me, but her brain wasn't so understanding.

Thorn was my last chance.

I stopped by his office in the middle of the day, knowing he would see me despite what he was doing. Luckily, I caught him in between meetings, and I was able to get into his office without a fuss.

Thorn looked just as displeased as ever to see me. We were always on opposites sides of the battlefield. There was only a very short period where we were truly allies. He didn't rise from his chair to greet me. He only looked thoroughly annoyed. "Because of you, I lost a great business opportunity. I'm not exactly thrilled to look at you."

"It was Titan's deal—so you didn't lose out on anything."

"She's going to be my wife. So what's hers is mine." He left his chair and came around the desk. He leaned against it and crossed his ankles. His arms folded over his chest. There wasn't a hint of friendliness in his eyes. "What the hell do you want, Hunt?"

This wasn't getting off to a good start. I doubted he would help me out under any circumstances. "I'm sure Titan told you about our conversation with Bruce Carol."

"Yes, the woman tells me everything," he snapped. "You forget that I've been her rock for the past decade. You've only been around for six months."

I ignored the insult. "I've done everything I can to convince her I never betrayed her. She won't listen to me. She's given up on me."

"About damn time."

Maybe this was a waste of time. "She told me you are going to propose on Saturday."

"Yeah, I am." He looked me right in the eye as he said it. "And if you do anything to interfere, I'm not going to hold back."

"I've never tried to interfere with her life."

"Hmm," he said sarcastically. "Then what are you doing now?"

"Talking."

"And what did you want to talk about?"

Judging from his attitude, this wasn't going to go anywhere. I didn't have a chance to make this right. I'd have to hope for some kind of miracle. "Don't ask her to marry you."

He rolled his eyes. "Unbelievable…"

"I can't prove it, but I've been telling the truth. I know how important she is to you. So if I'm the man she's supposed to be with, you would want her to be with me. Thorn, I'm that man."

"No, you aren't." He left the front of the desk and circled back to his chair. "You should just disappear. You've caused us nothing but grief since you came into our lives. I miss her old lovers, the guys I've never met."

I swallowed the jealousy all the way down my throat. Picturing her with anyone else but me made me sick.

"If you love the girl, just leave her alone. Call it off so she can move on."

"It's because I love her that I can't leave, Thorn. This is all a huge mistake."

He slipped his hands into his pockets and looked out the window. "I'm not having this conversation anymore, Hunt. I'm marrying Titan, and we're going to have the lives we planned out. You had your chance, but you blew it. With me, she'll never know pain. She'll never know betrayal. The greatest heartache she's ever known has been because of you." He shook his head and didn't turn around to look at me. "Get out of my office, Hunt. I never want to see your face again. Go back to being the dirty secret that you are."

THE NEXT FEW days were long and lonely.

I didn't hear from Hunt. When I told him I would say yes to Thorn's proposal, he turned white. His usually tanned skin paled. The color of his eyes dulled. Instead of arguing with me, he walked out of my penthouse without saying a word to me.

I hadn't heard from him since.

Maybe he didn't want to continue our arrangement once I was engaged. Maybe it was too difficult for him, to see me wear another man's ring. Or maybe his plan backfired, and now there was no reason to stay.

I really didn't know.

When Saturday arrived and I still hadn't heard from him, I knew he was gone. It was his quiet way of excusing himself from our arrangement. A conversation wasn't necessary because his silence was enough.

I put on a navy blue gown that had arrived at my penthouse a few hours before. I did my hair in big curls, wore diamond earrings that would match the ring Thorn was about to give me, and I wore a diamond necklace with a circular pendant in the middle. We'd been planning this for a long time, and I should feel excited.

But I didn't feel an ounce of joy.

When I fell in love with Hunt, I pictured the way he would ask me to marry him. I pictured the white dress I would wear to our wedding. I imagined myself pregnant with his child, heavy around the stomach as I waddled through the house. I picture a life full of laughter, good sex, and happiness.

But that was never going to happen.

I was marrying Thorn. We would love each other, but we would never love one another passionately. I would have my partners, and he would have his. We'd have sex, but it wouldn't be often. He would be my best friend in the world, my closest confidant.

But he would never give me butterflies.

He would never make me weak.

I knew I had to accept that and move on.

The light over the elevator lit up, and the doors opened.

Thorn was here to pick me up.

Except it wasn't Thorn. It was Hunt.

He walked into my apartment in jeans that hung low on his hips and a t-shirt that fit nicely against his chest. His eyes roamed over my appearance, taking in the diamonds in my ears and the curves of my tight dress. He walked up to me, his broad shoulders shifting with every step he took.

As always, I held my breath. Anytime he was near, I wasn't myself. I wasn't so confident, wasn't so cold.

He stopped directly in front of me, invading my personal space like he owned all of it. He refrained from touching me, but I could feel his hands all over my body. I could feel his fingers in my hair, feel them at the back of my neck. "When he asks you to marry him, you're going to think of me."

The statement was so blunt that it took me a moment to digest.

"And if you're going to think of me, then I should be the one asking you."

When I looked into that unbelievably handsome face, it was hard to resist. There was nothing I wanted more than to see him give me a ring then return home to a night of kissing and touching. "I wish you were, Hunt..."

"Then let me be the one."

I bowed my head, unable to look at the plea in his

eyes. "It's over. You didn't give me enough to believe you, enough to trust you. I said no to your father because I couldn't betray you. But now I need to do the best thing for me. If you can't accept that, then we should stop seeing each other."

A quiet sigh escaped his lips. "Baby..."

"I mean it, Hunt."

"I don't want to stop seeing you."

"Then we need to stop talking about this. Can you do that?"

I didn't get an answer, but he looked into my eyes as acknowledgment.

I stepped around him and grabbed my clutch. "You should go. He's going to be here any minute..."

Hunt walked back to the elevators and hit the button with his finger. He turned his eyes back to me and watched me as he waited for the elevator. His eyes scanned over my face like they usually did, blanketing me with affection and love. The muscles of his throat shifted as he swallowed. The elevator doors opened, but he didn't step inside right away.

He kissed me instead. It was a soft kiss, full of restrained passion that he couldn't allow to break free. His fingers dug into my hair slightly so he wouldn't mess up my curls. There was no tongue, but his lips felt perfect against my mouth. When he ended the embrace, he kept his face close to mine. "Thorn is a lucky man." He dropped his hand and walked into the elevator. He hit the button for the lobby but wouldn't make eye contact with me. He stared at the buttons as he waited for the doors to close.

Slowly, they came to the middle until he was gone from sight.

And then he left.

---

"YOU LOOK BEAUTIFUL." THORN SMILED AT ME BEFORE he leaned in and kissed me on the cheek. It was a special embrace, affection that we never showed unless people were watching. It was nice, an ode to things to come.

"Thanks. You look nice too."

"Well, I always look nice." He smiled before he grabbed my hand and pulled me into the elevator. We rode it to the bottom just as Hunt had five minutes earlier. Thorn escorted me to the back seat of his car, and the driver pulled into traffic.

Thorn looked out the window and watched the lights go by.

I tried not to think about Hunt.

"Everything alright?" he asked without looking at me.

"Yeah."

He turned his head toward me. "You're sure? Because speak now or forever hold your peace."

There was nothing waiting for me with Hunt. Nothing but hesitation and uncertainty. I remained loyal to him even though I didn't have to, but I had to put myself first. I had to do the right thing for myself because he wouldn't do the right thing by me. "I'm sure."

A handsome smile spread across his face. "I was hoping you'd say that."

Silence fell again, and Thorn fished out his phone. He took care of a few messages, and by the time he was done, we pulled up in front of the restaurant. He got out first and then helped me out, his hand steady on mine.

When I thought about spending my life with Thorn, I didn't have a single fear in the world. I knew he would always be honest with me, not feeding me lies to hide his true nature. He would only show me the respect that I deserved. He would be affectionate, loyal. He would be a great friend and a wonderful husband. He was a handsome man, so I knew our children would be beautiful. He would be a wonderful father, a great family man. I was a lucky woman to find such a great man. We wouldn't know passionate love, but I could always find that elsewhere.

He guided me into the restaurant, and at a special table right next to the window were his parents and some of our friends. They all knew what was going to happen, but they had no idea that I knew as well.

Hopefully, I was believable.

Hopefully, Hunt wouldn't haunt me for the rest of the night.

Brett sat across from me at the table inside the bar. The lights were low, and people were talking over the music. The TVs around the room showed a playback of the game that aired hours ago. I skipped the beer and went straight for something stronger.

An Old Fashioned.

It was a cruel punishment.

Brett didn't hide his stare. He looked at me openly, the way only a brother could. He violated my personal space because he was allowed to by the connection of our DNA. He glanced at my nearly empty glass before he looked at me again. "I'm sorry, man."

I could hear the compassion in his tone, knowing he really meant every word he said. He didn't like to see me down on my luck, disappointed by the hand that was dealt to me. I never let anyone see me like this, but I didn't care anymore. "I know."

"What are you going to do now?"

My fingers wrapped around the glass, feeling the condensation that formed on the surface. "The same thing I was doing before."

"Which is?"

"I haven't given up on her."

Brett couldn't hide the look of pity he flashed my way. "Come on, man…"

"I won't give up on her." My eyes shifted to the TV in the corner just when the channel changed and a news story broke out.

A reporter came on the air. "It's official. Thorn Cutler asked his longtime girlfriend, Tatum Titan, to marry him. The engaged couple was seen having dinner with friends and family at Rio's." Photographs were shown of Thorn on one knee in front of the table. The diamond on the band was enormous, sparkling even through the photograph.

She said yes.

I looked at her face in the picture. She smiled down at Thorn, but her eyes were wet with emotion. I knew the wetness wasn't from happiness, wasn't from joy at the thought of a lifetime of bliss with Thorn.

I knew she was thinking about me.

A few minutes later, it returned to the game.

Brett didn't say anything, but his pity increased. His eyes fell in sadness, knowing the images we just saw were knives straight to my heart.

As if nothing had happened, I picked up my glass and drank the rest of the contents.

Brett continued to stare.

"I know I'll get her back." It would take them at least nine months to plan the wedding that would be a performance for the world to see. I had plenty of time to fix this, to make things right. She was still mine as far as I was concerned.

Brett hadn't touched his beer once. It'd been sitting there for minutes, growing lukewarm.

"I may not have any proof, but I believe in what we have. I know she'll take a leap of faith. I know she'll give me another chance even if I don't have anything to exonerate myself. She's scared and doesn't want to get hurt again, but she'll take that risk for me. I know she will."

"Why are you so certain?"

I couldn't explain to Brett the depth of our connection, the intensity of our feelings. I'd never been a romantic guy, but I knew real love when I saw it. What we had was the kind of power that could conquer an entire world. The right language didn't exist for me to convey exactly what we shared. But I could feel it in my heart. "Because that woman loves me with everything she has. And I love her in the exact same way."

## ALSO BY VICTORIA QUINN

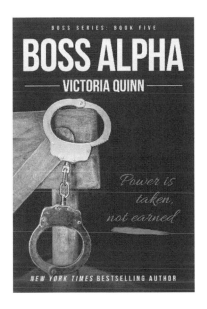

Order Now

# MESSAGE FROM HARTWICK PUBLISHING

As insatiable romance readers, we love great stories. But we want original romance novels that have something special - something we remember even after we turn the last page. That's how Hartwick Publishing came to be.

We promise to bring you beautiful stories that are unlike any other on the market - and that already have millions of fans.

With several New York Times bestselling authors, Hartwick Publishing is unparalleled. Our focus is not on the authors, but on you, the reader!

Join Hartwick Publishing by signing up for our newsletter!

As a thank you for joining our family, you will receive the first volume of the Obsidian Series (Black Obsidian) for free directly into your email inbox!

Also, be sure to follow us on Facebook so you know when the next great romance novel is released.

- Hartwick Publishing